Vixens of Horror

VINTAGE EDITION

Curated by
LISA VASQUEZ

Edited by
Lisa Lee Tone

Featuring stories by

Cassandra Jones
Megan Stockton
Angelique Fawns
Candace Nola
Christine Morgan
Chantell Renee
Caitlin Marceau
Miracle Austin
Rebecca Evanesky

Table of Contents

Foreword

ALL OF YOUR FREEDOMS ARE DUE TO THE SACRIFICES OF THE PAST.

While we give thanks to our military veterans for keeping our country free, we must also give thanks for the everyday heroes who spoke up in spite of threats of violence, incarceration, societal exile, and bullying.

The women of the 1950s are no exception.

The 1950s presented a society rife with gender roles, where women were expected, *and groomed*, to focus on home-making and motherhood. To make matters worse, women were limited in reproductive rights such as birth control unless their husband gave them *permission*.

Women were limited in career opportunities and faced workplace discrimination. There was an increase in domestic violence, which was often hidden. With few resources available compared to what we have available today, women were experiencing abusive situations with no hope for escape. Sexual harassment was swept under the carpet with restricted recourse.

Social expectation was an immense pressure placed on the shoulders of women to conform to femininity and propriety, impacting personal choices and freedoms.

The sad realization about all of these threats our mothers and grandmothers faced is that they are still present and prevalent today. While the landscape has evolved, addressing these challenges requires ongoing efforts to promote gender equality, awareness, and policy changes. Advances in women's rights have been made, but there is still work to be done to ensure true equality in every aspect of our lives.

In the world of art, there is a freedom of expression. They say a picture is worth a thousand words. *Expression,* in the world of art, will always surpass words. Art in all its forms gives a voice to a million souls who have been oppressed and underrepresented, are fearful of repercussions, have been unseen and unheard, and those who have experienced pain so deep it can never be spoken out loud. Art gives us a connection beyond verbalization; it transcends language and cultural divide.

Vixens of Horror is not only about a small genre of fiction in the indie community. It is about women who add volume to a cause while forming a safe place to open up about the issues we face every day. There is strength in numbers, and we'll start with a few until a few become many.

Vixens of Horror: Vintage Edition is a collection of stories focused on women living in the 1950s who suffocated under a sea of oppression only to find their voice through channeled rage. These stories are written by some of the strongest women I've met in our community, who have built their own empires through hard work, dedication, and pure grit. Some of the authors are making their debut and sit among examples of what it takes to be a woman writing in Horror today. It is my hope to continue bringing collections that touch on serious subjects with a tongue-in-cheek approach. Horror is designed to make the reader uncomfortable, so be prepared to squirm. They say beauty is skin deep, but we'll be digging deeper for the squelch and juiciest parts.

Consider this volume an homage to the beautiful women in the not-so-distant past who have forged a foundation for us today. Women like:

- Simone de Beauvoir, who laid the foundation for feminist philosophy and examined the social construction of womanhood with her book *The Second Sex*.
- Maya Angelou, whose powerful autobiography, *I Know Why the Caged Bird Sings*, in 1969, addressed issues of race, gender, and resilience. While outside of the 1950 range, her numerous contributions made her an influential figure in the civil rights movement.
- Rachel Carson, both a scientist and author, who wrote *Silent Spring* and raised awareness about environmental issues.
- Rosa Parks, the "Mother of the Civil Rights Movement," who refused to give up her *damn* seat. Overall Culp Hobby, who was appointed the first Secretary of Health, Education, and Welfare in 1953 and went on to become a trailblazer in government leadership roles, showed us that women could be more than a secretary and office barista.
- Pauli Murray, civil rights and women's rights activist, lawyer, and author, whose dedication laid the groundwork for legal arguments against gender-based discrimination.
- Dorothy Pitman Hughes and Gloria Steinem,

who were active in civil rights activities and later had highly influential roles.

We are thankful for the non-Caucasian women who stood against all adversity and threat of racism to open up the way for us:

- Ella Baker, who worked with the NAACP and the Southern Christian Leadership Conference. Dorothy Height, who was president of the National Council of Negro Women, continuing her work for decades.
- Celia Cruz, "The Queen of Salsa" and Cuban-American singer who became a symbol of Latin music and culture.
- Patsy Mink, a Japanese American lawyer and politician who was elected to the US House of Representatives in 1956, becoming the first woman of color and first Asian American women elected to Congress.
- Maria Tallchief, who was a Native American woman of the Osage Nation, ballerina, and first Native American to hold the rank of prima ballerina in the New York City Ballet.
- Zara Neale Hurston, author of *Their Eyes Were Watching God*, who continued to influence African American literature in the 1950s.

Without the fearlessness of these women who had the *balls* to stand up to all odds, face terrifying backlash, and possibly be shunned from their own families, we would not have opportunities we have today.

As a woman in the dawn of my 50s, I look at where I've come from and where I'm heading. A few of the proudest achievements in my life has been having my words published, and to help other women do the same. I want to teach the new blood to be fierce and fearless and to give *back* to other women. Our sex is a highly competitive one, but there is room for all of us to **rise**.

I hope you enjoy the fear brought to you by the women of this collection, served on a cold silver platter.

Lisa Vasquez
    CEO Stitched Smile Publications
    Co-Owner and Editor-in-Chief of Memento Mori Ink Magazine
    Author and Award-Winning Cover Artist
    Founder of Vixens of Horror
    The Unsaintly Queen

Twisted Angel

CASSANDRA JONES

Chapter One

She made her way through the house, making sure everything was in its place. That's how things were supposed to be. Even though her husband tended to take things way too far. He liked to control everything she did.

She knew she was supposed to be the perfect wife and keep him happy. Didn't she deserve to be happy too? He made sure that never happened.

Karen made her way to the living room. The fire was making the living room comfortable. That was a good thing. Richard hated when the house was chilly. It had been staying colder in the evenings.

She had to get the dishes finished before he came home. She had been cleaning the entire house all day. Richard had told her it needed to be spotless when he returned from work.

Looking at the clock on the wall, she sighed. There wasn't much time left before he would come through the door. That was if he came home on time. He had been late almost every night over the last month.

Karen dried the plates before putting them in the cabinet. Her husband claimed he was working late on the nights he came in hours later than his usual time. She knew the truth of where he was spending his time. She had to keep that to herself because it would only make him angry at her.

She didn't want to do that. Richard could be mean when he was angry. That's why she never asked where he was after he left work. It wasn't like he would tell her the truth anyway.

Sitting at the table, she took a drink of her coffee. Would he be angry tonight? He seemed to be unhappy a lot lately. She had no idea what she had done wrong, and he refused to tell her.

Richard was a doctor, so she knew he might be called away unexpectedly. He may also need to stay late at work. Although she knew that wasn't the case. It wasn't his work keeping him away from their home.

He would never admit to seeing those other women. She had seen him with them in town. Everyone knew about his secret rendezvous with those women. She was sure everyone thought she was too blind to see the truth or she just didn't care.

Maybe she really didn't anymore. She was tired of living the way they were. She was tired of being taken for granted and mistreated. Tired of the fighting. Most of all, she was just tired.

Karen went into the living room again. She hadn't heard Richard's car pull into the driveway yet. That meant she had at least a few more minutes to enjoy the quiet.

He usually called when he was going to be late. She hadn't heard from him since he left for work that morning. He may be on his way home now. She could keep watching for him. It wasn't as if she had any other work to do in the house.

She spent the next half hour standing at the window watching for his car to pull up. Once again, his dinner would be cold when he came in. That would start another fight between the two of them.

She could always reheat the food when he came, but he would still be mad at her for it. He was always finding things to complain about. It was like his favorite thing to do was yell at her.

Making her way through the house, she double-checked everything. Going into the bathroom, she splashed some water on her face. Would he be in a bad mood when he got home? He was rarely ever in a good mood anymore.

She knew his work wasn't easy, but she also knew he took time for himself. He made sure he got his alone time at work as well as at home. She wasn't sure why he had even been interested in marrying anyone.

He preferred to be by himself most of the time. At least he did when he was at home. Maybe she was the problem? He didn't seem to want to be around her unless he had to. That was no way to live.

Karen went back to the living room just as Richard pulled into the driveway. She was about to find out what kind of mood he was in tonight. She hoped he was in a good mood, but that probably wasn't true.

She watched him come in, slamming the door behind him. He was in a horrible mood. The rest of the night would be an awful one.

"What are you staring at?" he yelled.

"Did you have a good day?" She forced a smile.

"Don't answer my question with a question." He sat down in his chair. "I hate when you do that."

"Do what?" Karen swallowed hard waiting for him to explode.

"You act like you're a perfect little wife." He raked a hand through his hair. "Everyone knows what you do when I'm at work. Where's my dinner?"

She went to the kitchen, grabbing his food and coffee. Maybe he would be happier after he ate. She doubted that would happen, though. He was never happy.

Things had changed so much over the last ten years. They were both excited about their marriage. Now it was simply a mistake to him. He had never loved her at all.

"Sit down and don't say anything else until I'm finished," Richard snapped at her.

Karen sat down on the sofa. She doubted they would talk about anything else tonight. He would eat his dinner, clean up, and go to bed. Just like he usually did.

He would be home from work tomorrow because he never worked on the weekends. If tonight was any indication, she knew how it would all go. She wasn't looking forward to it.

Chapter Two

Karen looked out the window into the backyard. Richard was sitting out there relaxing. He hadn't spent any time with her all morning. He had refused to even speak to her at breakfast. She wished she knew why he acted this way. He always blamed it on her.

How was she supposed to be a good wife if her husband wanted nothing to do with her? He had put up these walls to keep her out. She didn't understand why he acted that way with only her. He treated everyone else like they were important to him.

She went back to the sink to finish the dishes. She could keep herself busy with housework. She would pretend he wasn't home. He was ignoring her anyway.

She heard him come in the back door. He set his glass on

the counter next to her. She refused to look at him. She could be just as childish as he was.

"I have some errands to run." Richard started to leave the room.

"Will you be back for lunch?" She turned to face him. "Or should I just wait until you get home to make something?"

"I don't know." He shook his head. "Look, I'll be back when I get back."

Karen watched him go out the door. She knew exactly where he was running to. One of his women must have wanted to see him, or maybe he wanted to see them. It shouldn't matter to her anymore. He was always going off with them.

He would come home so they could argue and go to bed. That was all he wanted her here for. She would let him yell at her until he ran out of energy. Then he would go to bed while she stood there looking dumbfounded.

Grabbing the glass from the counter, she threw it against the wall. She didn't want to live this way. She wanted someone who made her happy. She needed someone who would treat her like a human being.

She hated him more every day. She felt the anger building up inside her. She wasn't letting him push her around any longer. This ended tonight.

She wasn't sure what she would do about it. She just knew she couldn't take the hate and abuse anymore. She shouldn't be treated like some kind of an animal in her own home. Her husband should love her. Richard couldn't even stand to look at her.

She went to the bedroom, grabbing her suitcase. She couldn't leave without him hunting her down. She had to find a way to stop him from doing that.

He wouldn't be home for hours, so she had time to come up with a plan. She should have done something a long time ago. Instead, she had taken the emotional abuse for years. It had eventually changed to him grabbing her arms or her hair. After a while, he had seemed to enjoy hurting her in other ways. She had the scars to prove it.

He didn't care what he used on her. His fists, belt, or even the broom. He only wanted her to feel the pain. It seemed to bring him some kind of sick pleasure. It made her want to do something worse to him.

She doubted that would happen. She wasn't the type of person to inflict pain on others, no matter what they did to her. Still, she had to do whatever it took to get away from him.

She might have to stay here for a few more days. She could make sure she had everything she would need. She didn't have to be in a rush. She wasn't even sure where she would go yet.

She hadn't spoken to her parents in about six years. They had tried to warn her about the man she married. Why hadn't she seen through his facade? That would have saved her a lot of tears and pain.

After packing her suitcase, she stuck it in the back of the closet. She knew he wouldn't notice it. She had to make sure his clothes were in the bathroom whenever he wanted to change. He didn't think he should waste time going through closets and drawers.

Karen went back to the kitchen so she could clean up the glass. She didn't want to give him anything else to be mad about later. She wished he would stay gone for a night or two.

That was not going to happen, though. He truly believed a man's home was his castle, and he ruled it with an iron fist. He let her know who was in charge of their home. He didn't care how much he hurt her.

She thought about giving her parents a call. They would be surprised to hear from her after all this time. Would they talk to her? She thought her father would tell her to never call again. Her mother might be a bit more understanding, though.

Karen picked the phone up, holding it to her ear. Why was she so afraid to speak to her own parents? She wasn't a child anymore. She needed to be strong. She wouldn't be able to leave Richard if she was cowering in a corner somewhere. She had to stop being so scared of the man. He wasn't going to stop until she stood up to him. At least, she hoped that would make him stop.

Karen looked out the window. When had it started raining? A flash of lightning lit up the sky, followed by a clap of thunder. This was perfect for the day they were having.

The weather matched her mood. It made her a bit edgy as well. She knew it wouldn't make Richard's mood any better. He hated when it stormed. He claimed it made it impossible to go outside for anything.

He really meant he couldn't get away from her. She could care less if he went outside and got struck by lightning. Maybe that would teach him to be nicer to her.

She was about to find out how he would react. She stood by the counter waiting for him to come in. It was time for their fight to start.

Chapter Three

He stood there staring at her. Why had he decided to come home? It wasn't like they would be talking about anything. He hated talking to his wife. She was the person he most wanted to get rid of.

Too bad his parents didn't want him to get a divorce. That was the only reason he stayed with her. She didn't deserve to have anyone love her. She wasn't worth anyone's time.

Richard shook his head. She hadn't said a word since he

came in. She hadn't met him at the door like she was supposed to. She knew better than that.

"What are you doing?" he yelled.

"Standing in the kitchen." Karen chewed on her lower lip.

Good. That meant she knew she was in trouble. She had to pay for her mistakes. She knew her place in his house. Why couldn't she get it through her head?

He didn't want to do things to punish her. She brought it on herself. She made him do these things to her. It wasn't his fault.

The thunder shook the windowpanes. Why did it have to storm? He really didn't like this kind of weather. It made his mood even more foul.

Her attitude made it worse. Why would she talk back to him? She was well aware of what that would bring about. When would she learn her lesson? He was getting tired of showing her what happened when she didn't obey him.

Richard slowly made his way towards her. He wanted to make her squirm a little. She deserved to feel the fear running up her spine. He loved when he made her cower in fear.

"Richard, what are you doing?" Karen backed against the sink.

"Are you supposed to be in the kitchen?" He grabbed her wrist. "You are supposed to be at the front door when I get home. You know that."

"I didn't know when you would be home." She swallowed hard. "Was I supposed to stand by the door all night?"

"Yes." Richard got in her face. "That is exactly what you do when I'm not home."

"When would I clean the house and cook dinner?" Karen asked, her voice barely a whisper.

"Don't talk back to me." He pushed her back against the sink.

He didn't care how much he hurt her. She didn't need his

mercy, and she wouldn't get it. She would feel his wrath. It was the only thing she would ever get from him.

He refused to show her any type of love. How could he love someone he hated so much? His parents knew how he truly felt about his wife. Of course, he had told them she was the one who caused all of their problems.

So what if that wasn't the truth? No one knew about their private lives. He made sure what happened in his house stayed in his house. Karen wouldn't tell anyone because she would only make him angry. Besides, he didn't let her talk to anyone other than him.

After tonight, he would make sure she never talked again. He would make sure she couldn't speak when he was through with her. He was going to have fun with her tonight.

He smiled, thinking about what he planned to do to her. She wouldn't know what hit her until it was too late. For now, he needed her out of his way. He had to get things ready for her.

Grabbing her hair, he pulled her to the closet. He pushed her inside, slamming the door. He had put a lock on the door just for this reason. He had locked her in there several times before. She couldn't get out no matter how hard she tried.

He made his way to the garage. He would need some rope. He might find something else in here he could use. He would give her an hour to think about what her actions would cause. She had been the one to disobey him. She had to pay for that.

Tonight would be the last time he taught her how to behave. He was done being so nice with her. From now on, she would be the perfect wife.

Chapter Four

Karen sat against the wall of the closet. She hated it when

he locked her in here. The last time, she had been left in here overnight. She wished she could take the door off the hinges.

What was he doing out there, anyway? She knew he was planning to do something to her. She had a feeling she had really made him furious this time.

How was she supposed to know when he would come home? Most of the time when he went out, he stayed gone until the next morning. She certainly couldn't stand by the door all night.

She wasn't going to make this easy for him. If he wanted to punish her, he had to fight her to do it. She was done being his punching bag. She wouldn't be his victim anymore. After tonight, he would have to find someone else to abuse.

She leaned her head against the wall. She had to find a way to end this. Her plan to leave might not work, since he came home before she could figure it all out. She had to think of something else.

What was he going to do? When was he going to do it? He was most likely making her think about it so she would be even more scared of him. She hated when he did this to her.

She could hear him making noise, so she knew he was still out there. She wasn't sure she wanted to know what he was up to. He was getting things ready for her punishment.

She jumped when he pulled the door open. He grabbed her hair, pulling her from the closet. Karen let him pull her back into the kitchen. There was no point fighting him. At least not yet. She had to bide her time until she could get away from him. That was the only way she would survive this night. She had to survive.

"I am so tired of telling you what you are supposed to do," he screamed in her face. "That ends tonight."

"What are you going to do?" She swallowed hard.

"You'll find out soon enough." Richard laughed. "We're going to have a little fun."

"Please don't do this," she begged him. "I'll do whatever you tell me."

"Shut up." He knocked her back into the counter.

Karen felt the pain shoot through her entire body. She stopped fighting to look around the room. That was when she noticed the rope on the table. That was a bad sign.

She could not let him tie her up. That would be her death sentence. She had to stop him now.

Karen noticed the knife on the counter. She needed to get her hands on it. If she had a weapon, he might back off. She had to say least try.

Richard turned toward the rope. She lunged for the knife at the same time. He turned back to face her so quickly she almost dropped it.

He tried to grab the knife from her hand. Karen swung her arm, catching his hand with the blade. He grabbed a dish towel.

"What are you doing?" Richard turned the water on. "I'll kill you for that."

"No, you won't." Karen stabbed him in the back. "You won't touch me ever again."

She kept stabbing him and stabbing him. She had put up with his abuse for so long. She kept all of her anger inside. She was letting all of that anger out now. Ten years' worth of abuse and hate.

Richard had stopped moving. Karen let the knife fall from her hand. She couldn't believe what she had done. She had to do something. She had stabbed her husband to death. She would get in trouble if anyone found out.

Karen grabbed the knife, wrapping it in a towel. She had to get rid of it. She hurried to the bedroom to get her suitcase. She put it in the backseat of the car along with the knife.

Going back into the house, she went to the bathroom. She quickly showered and changed, making sure to take her dirty clothes with her. She would get rid of them with the knife.

Before getting in the car, Karen took all of the money from Richard's wallet. She had to get away from here. She had no idea where to go. She drove to the river first. Grabbing the knife and her clothes, she tossed them in the water.

She stood there for a while watching the water. She was finally free of her nightmare. She didn't have to live in fear any longer.

Karen got back in the car, smiling. She was leaving town and never looking back. She had stopped being afraid and finally took control of her life. No one would ever control her again.

No Place for a Man

by Megan Stockton

The house was clean, top-to-bottom. Janet had even stood precariously on a kitchen chair to dust the corners of the ceilings. She had ironed all of her husband's shirts, and the ironing board and steam iron was sitting in the living room to cool. She cleaned when she was nervous, like a good housewife. That's all she had ever really wanted to be: a good wife. She wanted to be productive even when she was stressed; she wanted to exude happiness even when she wasn't happy herself. She felt very sterile, clean, put-together like her house, even if she wasn't sure she was happy all the time.

This uncertainty had started with book club, something so unassuming and yet had become so dangerous. She and Steven had been married six months ago and bought the picturesque home in suburbia, and Janet had been eager to bond with the other ladies on the street. Until book club.

"So you'll be out late tonight?" Steven asked, newspaper rustling in his hands as he flipped through.

Janet flinched, folding the rag in her hand carefully before laying it on the countertop. "Oh, yes. Cynthia said we have a lot to discuss with this book."

"A lot to discuss? What kind of book is it?"

"It's a ... thriller."

He chuckled, putting the paper down neatly and stalking slowly around the counter with a grin. "A thriller? With murder and intrigue and bad guys?"

She couldn't help but giggle at him, putting her fingers to her lips as she tried to back away around the other side of the counter.

"Yes, murder and all that ..."

He lunged for her, and she squealed, wrapped in his arms instantly as he planted a gentle kiss on her lips. Janet could have melted into him. She was covered in the warmth of both comfort and desire. She smiled at him—the smallest, meekest gesture—as she slipped her fingertips and palm across the smooth skin of his cheek. He always kept a clean, close shave. His thick, auburn hair was always slicked back and styled immaculately, and the blend of his aftershave, cologne, and hair product was to die for. Steven was perfect, and that was what made tonight so damn hard.

Moments later, she was watching him pull the shining Ford coupe out of the driveway ... and then she saw the light in the living room at Cynthia's house illuminate. In the window, curtains parted to reveal four figures standing there in their dresses. Cynthia stood in the center of them, hands folded proper at her waist. To her left, a woman with black curls smiled and raised a hand to wave. It was time, and they would not wait on Janet all night.

She took several deep breaths, smoothing her hair and checking her makeup in the mirror before she headed out the door and across the street with the novel tucked against her breast. Every house in the neighborhood was identical in shape and size, and only varied by color. Janet and Steven's house was mint green, Cynthia's was pastel pink, and both Cathy and Robin lived in butter-yellow houses.

Cynthia had the door open before Janet had closed the white gate behind her. She was alone there, smiling as she gestured for Janet to hurry on. Janet's ankle wavered on the edge of the sidewalk as she hurried towards and then into the house. Her stomach tied into nervous knots as she thought about the confrontation she was about to have. Instead of allowing Cynthia to start talking, going through her usual spiel about where the sweet tea was, what snacks were available, and apologizing about any mess ... Janet quickly approached the difficult subject, trying to be proactive.

"Cyndi, I've been really thinking about all of this ... I just don't think—"

"I'm going to stop you right there, Janet. We've been waiting for you, patiently I'd say. I've got something to show you ladies."

Cathy and Robin hovered in the entry to the living room, and Janet nervously fell in line as they followed Cynthia down the hallway. Janet had been down this hall as far as the guest bathroom, but she knew the layout was identical to her own home. The only other rooms down that hall would be the study or spare bedroom, and the master bedroom and attached bath. As Cynthia passed up the guest bathroom and office and turned left into the master bedroom, Janet hesitated in the doorway. It felt ... wrong to enter someone else's bedroom. That was a sacred space, as far as Janet was concerned. Of course, she was the youngest and mostly recently married of the four women. When Robin caught her pinky, pulling her inside with a smile, Janet hesitantly followed them into the master bath.

The five women stood circled around the pink bathtub, where the naked body of Cynthia's husband rested in four inches of bloody water. Janet's blood ran cold. Out of the corner of her eye, she saw Cathy put a hand to her mouth, and Robin squeaked in her throat in surprise. Janet wrapped her arms around her stomach nervously, hands brushing over her arms, where her skin was so cool and covered in goosebumps that it felt crisp and frosty.

"You did it," Cathy breathed. "You actually did it."

Cynthia was composed as always and put a hand up as though she were presenting something. "Of course I did. This is what we talked about, wasn't it? This is what we all wanted, right?"

Janet wanted to speak up, but her voice caught in her throat. Robin made another sound in her throat, this one more like a nervous giggle that droned off into a hum, then she spoke in the silence.

"How did you do it?"

Her voice was low, nearly a whisper. It was quieter than the slow drip of the faucet that sent ruddy ripples across the surface of the water. Everyone turned to look at her, and Janet was alarmed by the look of excitement and curiosity in her eyes. She was more shocked by the smile on her lips than the dead man submerged in the tub.

"Can we sit down somewhere?" Cathy asked, putting a hand to her temple. "While we discuss this?"

Cynthia ignored Cathy, directing her question straight to Robin. "I slit his throat with a straight razor. I was trying to decide how to do it since our last meeting. I just couldn't find the right time, then he asked me to help him shave. He tilted his head back into my lap, and I cut through it ... Just like a crisp apple in the summer. Just like making an apple pie."

Their book club had turned sinister months ago, when the ladies had started discussing some of the stupid things their husbands did. It started innocent enough but quickly turned into all of the gruesome ways they imagined they could kill their husbands. They talked about how much better off they'd

24

be without their husbands, how much happier, and how much more free. Janet didn't really agree with them, not really. She had said as much, multiple times, but she also desired to fit in so much.

"I thought about poisoning Alan," Cathy admitted, voice still so small and quiet. "I think that would be easier for me."

"Too slow," Cynthia dismissed with a wave.

"What if we helped each other do it?" Robin suggested. "It would be easier for the three of us to take them out together, one at a time. We don't have much time now because they'll all start to wonder where Patrick is. You could only lie so long about it."

Janet backed away from the group. "I can't do this. I love Steven. I *love* him."

"Oh, you're so young. All men are the same," Cynthia assured her.

Robin chimed in: "All they want is sex, food, and their house cleaned. We're slaves."

"Steven isn't like that. He helps me around the house, he cooks dinner, and we've never even ... We've never ..."

They all blinked at her. Even Cynthia seemed perplexed. "You've never what?"

Janet's face flushed, heat flooding her cheeks, ears, and eyes. She thought she might cry from embarrassment.

"You've never had sex with your husband?" Robin asked.

"No," Janet stammered. "He said it just isn't time yet and we have our entire lives. He's ... touched me, you know."

Now she sounded like some teenage girl talking to her friends after prom. She wished she could have melted straight into the floor. This wasn't a conversation she ever wanted to have with her peers, or with anyone. None of this was anyone's business, and she shouldn't have to explain or defend her sex life to anyone ... even her lack of one.

"Oh, honey." Cynthia put on a pitying face that made

Janet want to slap her. "If he isn't getting it from you ... Well, you know he's getting it from someone else. I would bet it's someone at the office. A temp or something. Just like Cathy's husband did last summer, remember that homewrecker, Cathy?"

Cathy murmured something like *how-could-I-forget* and looked down at the tile between their feet. Janet's chill had turned to numbness, and now the only ice she felt sat squarely in her gut. Was Steven really cheating on her? Did he think she would be inadequate? Or worse, was he not attracted to her? She thought about the way he would sometimes slip his fingers up her dress: soft fingertips tracing along her inner thigh, and the way he knew exactly what to do and how to do it. Too experienced, she now thought. She thought of the way that he would never let her reciprocate, always shyly pushing her hand away when she tried to unbuckle his belt. Was he so repulsed by her?

"So that settles it then," Cynthia said with a smile. "We'll ... clean up this mess *together,* then we will get rid of your husbands *together.*"

"Steven won't be home until later," Janet insisted.

"Well, then. We'll just hit your house last. Now, I've got a couple of tools in the garage and a flowerbed begging for fertilizer. Let's get to it, ladies! Chop, chop. Oh." She giggled. "I'm so funny, I didn't even realize the humor in that at first."

No one laughed.

Cynthia reached her porcelain white hand into the murky bathwater to pull the drain before she left to retrieve the tools. In her absence, the three women stood quietly, surrounded by the gurgling sound of the tub's draining pipes.

Janet leaned in towards Cathy and whispered feverishly, "You aren't really going to go through with this are you, Cathy? You aren't really going to kill Alan?"

Cathy's cheeks blushed, and she reached up to pull a

strand of straw-colored hair down to cover her reddening cheeks. "I can't stand him, Janet. You don't know what it's like. Cynthia is right ... It's like living with an animal. An animal that thinks *you* are a lesser animal."

"Robin?" Janet pleaded.

Honestly, Robin being homicidal didn't really surprise Janet. The dark-headed woman smiled, curls bobbing as she shook her head. She didn't have the opportunity to prod further, as Cynthia returned with outfits for all three of them and tools. She handed each of them a pair of elbow-length gloves and a rain jacket. Robin was given a mallet, Cathy a small ax, Cynthia kept a hand saw for herself, and she handed Janet a shovel.

"You can go ahead and start digging holes in the flower bed out back. One big one, several small ones."

Janet was dumbfounded, white-knuckled grip on the shovel in her hands. She watched as they huddled around the bathtub and Cynthia instructed them with the quiet patience of a school teacher. Robin broke the long bones with a mallet, the sounds of dull *thwack* turning into the crisp crunching of bone fragments beneath the bruising and swelling tissue. Cathy and Cynthia set to cutting the limbs in half at the breaks that Robin made, and Janet was drawn to the oozing black beads of blood adorning the man's pallid body like shimmering, wet diamonds.

She had to peel her eyes away, covering her mouth as she retreated from the room and went into the backyard. She took out her stress on the ground, digging into the soft soil with the shovel head as she waited. The ground felt plush and forgiving, delicate. Tears streamed down her face as she tried to channel the same anger that the other women must have felt towards the men. She imagined all of the things they said about Steven were true; she tried to imagine that it was all true ...

And she still couldn't do it. She dropped the shovel,

sprinting through the backyard to the gate. She passed through and looked over her shoulder in paranoia. When she turned back around, she saw the baby blue Ford parked in front of her house, and she stopped in the road, heart fluttering in her throat. A panic set in as she heard voices and laughter from behind her. They were going to notice that she was gone, and they were going to notice that Steven was back home. What was he doing home?

She kicked off her shoes, leaving them abandoned in the street as she clutched the bottom of her dress and the raincoat and ran the rest of the distance to her home, swinging the door open with shaking hands. She could smell the savory aroma of food coming from the kitchen as she locked the door behind her.

Steven came around the corner to meet her, smiling broadly. "Honey, what are you doing here? I was going to surprise you with dinner, but it's still got a few hours ... What are you wearing?"

"Steven, why are you here?" Janet could feel the cold sensation of fear creeping back into her body. Her head beaded with sweat, and she fully realized she was still wearing the raincoat and long cleaning gloves.

"Are you guys having some kind of costume party?" He leaned to the side, looking out the window. She turned and saw Robin, Cynthia, and Cathy striding across the road with their tools in their hands. They were covered in splatters of red. They wore smiles on their faces that Janet could only think of as psychotic. Unhinged.

"Steven, I need you to listen to me very carefully. We have to get out of here somehow. They're going to kill you. They want me to kill you."

"They what?" Steven's smile had faded now, but he didn't seem scared. He didn't believe her yet. She walked forward, taking the knife from the kitchen counter. It still smelled like onions, and tomato seeds clung to the surface. When it was in her hand, Steven took a step backwards. "Janet, put that down."

"You don't understand, sweetie," she said, voice cracking as she started to cry.

A rapid knocking made both of them jump.

"Janet, darling. We're here to help you clean. Won't you be a darling and let us in?" Cynthia's voice was calm, followed by the giggle of Robin.

"I need to know." Janet sniffled. "Are you cheating on me?"

The knife in her hand started to shake. Did it matter? She didn't want to kill Steven, even if he was unfaithful. They could work through this. They were young; they could do better together. They could work it out.

"What is going on, Jan?" Steven hadn't retreated but instead was making a slow and steady approach. "Please talk to me."

"Are you cheating on me?" Her voice was louder this time, and he paused.

"Of course not. I would never—"

"Why don't you want to have sex with me?" She felt the embarrassment again, face red and hot. She couldn't stop the snot and tears now, reaching up with the back of her gloved hand to wipe at her nose and almost stabbing herself in the eye in the process.

"This isn't the time to talk about this." All of the color had drained from Steven's face as he motioned to the door behind her. "What are they doing here?"

"We have to talk about this now, Steven. They're wanting me to kill you. They've already cut Patrick up into itty-bitty pieces, Steven. I have to kill you or they're going to kill us both. I need to know. I *need* you to tell me the truth now so we can try to get out of this together."

Steven didn't respond, but his spine stiffened. He reached up and loosened his tie, then started to unbutton his shirt. Janet was puzzled, brow furrowing and causing her tears to spill more freely. She watched as he unbuttoned it completely to reveal a white undershirt.

"I'm not saying that I wasn't wrong. I'm not saying that it wasn't wrong. I know it was wrong to hide this from you, but I just wasn't ready. I fell in love with you too fast, and I was too afraid. I just wanted to pretend a little while, just in case you ... Just in case you ..."

He had unbuckled his belt now, reaching down into his pants and retrieving a pair of wadded up socks, tossing them to the floor between them. Janet realized now that he wasn't wearing a shirt under his button up, but thin strips of fabric were wrapped around his upper torso. She watched as he unfastened his pants with shaking and fumbling fingers.

"Steven, stop."

He stopped, and she walked over to him, arm with the knife dropped down to her side. He didn't seem afraid, even when she clutched the weapon in her hand. She put her free hand on his cheek and stood on her tiptoes to kiss him on his soft lips. There was something that had always felt like home about kissing him. No matter where they were, she felt grounded.

"I don't care. Let's just ..."

She took a deep breath, mind reeling. "Let's kill these bitches."

Steven swallowed nervously but nodded at her. "I'll get the car keys and—"

Shattering glass had them both ducking. Janet squealed, dropping the knife and retreating into Steven's arms. He clutched her against him, staring slack-jawed at Cynthia as she put her arm through the broken glass, reaching over to unlock the door.

"Get in the bedroom and lock the door," he demanded quietly, grabbing the knife that Janet had dropped.

"No. You're outnumbered," she insisted, pulling at his loosened sleeve.

The door opened fully, and the three women stood there with smiles, like fairytale witches who wore yellow cloaks and gloves and used gardening tools to murder the innocent. Cynthia faked a pouty lip, shaking her head.

"So disappointed in you, Janet," she cooed. "I knew you didn't have it in you, but I didn't think you'd stand between us and what we have to do. This is just no place for a man. The world will be such a better place without them. Imagine ... what a perfect world it will be. A *utopia*."

She remained standing still, but Cathy and Robin came around each side of her as though they had choreographed this grand routine. Janet rushed into the living room, retrieving her steam iron and launching it through the air. It collided with Cathy's face, but just barely. She stumbled backwards, clutching her face and dropping the hatchet she carried in her hand.

"Oh, fudge!" she snarled, blood pouring between her fingers as she tried to keep her brow attached to her forehead. It hung there, and the skin around it flushed purple. She dropped to the ground and fumbled for the ax with her free hand, then lunged at Steven with another growl.

Janet saw Steven dodge the sloppy swing, and then she retreated into the living room to find something else to use as a weapon. Robin was coming for her, skipping through the kitchen with the mallet in her hands. Janet tried to keep an eye on Steven as he performed a deadly dance with Cathy. Cynthia still hadn't budged, still standing there in the doorway, waiting.

She almost didn't see Robin come at her with the hammer, swinging so hard that she missed Janet's narrowly ducking head and struck the stone mantle. Shards of rock flew through the air, and Robin clutched her elbow from the pain of the impact. Janet jerked the fire poker free, causing the rest of the tools to clatter across the floor. She jabbed forward with it, hitting Robin in the stomach but apparently not hard enough to puncture the flesh. Her pink blouse ripped, but her abdomen did not. The skin there was angry, puckering as though it were suddenly too full, but it did not bleed.

Robin swung with the hammer again, this time hitting Janet in the shoulder when she tried to duck out of the way again. It hurt. It hurt *so bad*, but at least she hadn't been hit in the head. She could feel a knot of pain welling up there, tingling sensations running down the length of her arm to her fingertips. She readjusted her grip and used it like a bat this time. Softball paid off.

She hit Robin in the head so hard that the pointed tip buried itself completely in her skull. She muttered something about butter in the fridge, and then she fell. She crumpled against the mantle, falling face first into the stone front and leaving a smear of blood and fractured teeth as she slid down into a heap with the iron still stuck in her scalp.

Janet clutched her shoulder and turned just in time to see Steven slice at Cathy's abdomen, but unlike Robin's, it didn't hold. Her stomach peeled open, and all of the contents poured out. Her guts spooled onto the floor, larger organs sagging and plopping atop the pile as Cathy slumped to the floor. She started wailing, screaming so loud that Steven dropped the knife and covered his ears. Cathy raked her organs closer to her, trying to stuff them back into the floppy maw of her torso, as she bawled like a siren into the air. Saliva poured out of her mouth, lips sagging.

Cynthia was leaving. She had turned tail and was walking across the yard at a brisk pace. Janet rushed across the room, grabbing the keys on the counter top and dragging Steven out the door. As they passed by Cathy, she clutched at them, begging them to help her even as her lips faded to the palest shade of blue.

Janet got into the driver's seat of the Ford, and Steven jumped over the door and into the passenger side. As Janet spun the tires, putting the car into reverse so quickly that the vehicle squealed, Steven jerked his seatbelt on nervously. She didn't think he'd ever worn a belt in the car; this was the first year they'd ever made the vehicles with the safety straps. It was just foreign, but Steven knew Janet was about to do something that definitely warranted an extra layer of protection. She put the car into drive and turned it sharply, pointing the grill at Cynthia as she fled across the road to her own home.

The car hit Cynthia and sent her flying through the air, splattering the windshield with blood from the impact. Steven reached over to turn on the wipers. Janet stopped the car long enough to look back and see the limp form of the neighbor unmoving. She pushed the gas again, heading down the neighborhood just at the speed limit.

"She deserved it," Janet breathed. "She deserved it, didn't she?"

Steven didn't respond at first, and she felt her stomach sink. She did what she had to do; they both did.

Then he reached over and put his hand on her knee, squeezing gently before letting his hand travel up her thigh. "The neighborhood road is a loop. Keep going, let's hit her again. Just in case."

Janet looked over at him in surprise, and then they laughed.

Lucy Deserves the Finer Things

by Angelique Fawns

Lucy furrowed her overplucked brows. She wasn't going to be able to pay her rent this month. The shabby studio wasn't much, but it was a roof over her head. She ran her hands over her satin nightgown—pink, frilly, and playing just the right amount of peek-a-boo. It hid all her saggy spots. The crepey skin on her chest wasn't as titillating as it had been twenty years ago, but the industrial underwire bra was still doing a good job. Hours on her backyard chaise lounge coated in baby oil had roasted her skin like a delicious fried chicken.

At sixty years old, it was hard to keep a sugar daddy. She was getting tired of the game. Bucking convention, she'd refused to be a housewife in her twenties. Vacuuming, cleaning, cooking. Let the tongues wag, she'd been a kept party girl. Her blood-red nails tugged on a bleach-blonde curl.

Oh, for the days she'd had half the town panting at her door. The hustle had been so much easier.

When could a lady let herself go a little? She deserved the finer things in life. Or at least a chance to put up her callused feet. Her pointy-toed stilettos were torture. When the sun dipped behind the endless pine forests of this tiny town, she'd rather wear her fuzzy mule slippers.

Damn stinking Doug. How dare he dump her? Who else was going to put up with the crusty old widower? She stomped her foot in frustration, her bunion screaming a protest.

They'd been dating for several months, and Mr. Money Bags was paying her bills. So, of course, she'd stopped heading to the Kroger for her shift checking out Wonder Bread. The long hours gave her cankles and that new stupid bunion. All her high school friends had avoided the labor market, but then again, they had to scrub toilets for beer-bellied spouses.

She pulled at a loose bit of lace on her nightie while going over the wanted ads in the local paper.

This stupid negligee had been a going-away gift from Doug. She'd opened the package, thinking: *This is it! He's going to ask me to move in with him.*

Instead, he dumped her.

But not before some sweating and grunting on her pull-out couch. A lame lay, then, "See you later, honey buns."

She got distracted from her fuming when she saw an interesting ad:

Looking for a paid female companion. Must be able to work nights.

Prefer AB- Blood type. $1 a week.

Apply in person after 9:00 p.m. at 666 Black Lotus Drive. Basement entrance.

It didn't pay much. Probably some decrepit old lady who needed help hitting the toilet. Perhaps the occasional blood transfusion? Not that she even knew her blood type. The red kind, she supposed.

It was almost 10:00 p.m. now.

Taking care not to aggravate the bursitis in her knees, she

pulled on a more suitable dress (pink, turtleneck, below the knees). Pressing her lips in a thin line, she looked at the five-inch winkle pickers by the front door. With a sigh, she took off her comfy slippers and slipped on the dreaded stilettos. Her legs were her best asset. She tried to show them off whenever she had the chance.

A quick dash of matching coral lipstick and she was ready to go. She grabbed her quilted handbag and flounced out the door.

It was a beautiful night. The moon cast a romantic glow over the trees of her cozy neighborhood. Why did her brain have to go to romance? Why couldn't the moon be eerie? Or something that didn't remind her of sucking face with a man?

She scowled and automatically avoided the cracks that could snag her heels. She was hoping that applying for a new job would distract her. But no. A mind worm was on an endlessly repeating track.

Dirty damn Doug.

Twinkie horndog dipshit.

The way he had broken up with her. Trying to be all sanctimonious.

He'd taken off his ballcap and crunched it to his chest. "Lucy, it's not you; it's me. I can't seem to get over my dead wife. I still visit her grave every Saturday night. I know you'll understand."

She understood he was tired of paying for her dinners.

She understood he'd been eyeing Vera at the Bingo Hall.

She understood she had to get a job now.

At least nothing was too far in this armpit town, so after twenty minutes of shuffling down the sidewalk in her high heels, she was at 666 Black Lotus Drive.

The bungalow windows were dark, and the entire street was quiet. No birds chirping. No raccoons rustling. Lucy walked around back. She stepped gingerly over the broken bits of concrete and went down the five steps to the solid oak back door.

She rapped on the door with her inch-long fake nails, and it swung open with a creak.

Lucy gave the door a hard shove, and the creaking ramped into a scream.

The door whacked someone on the other side.

A grumbly voice came from behind the heavy wood slab. "For the love of Satan, that was my forehead."

She peeked her head around and saw a roundish man, coated in mud and wearing an orange nylon Speedo bathing suit. He was lying on the hall floor, grunting, his hand on his forehead.

She didn't help him up, her eyes bugging at the gothic thrift store decor. Oil lamps lined a short hall that led to one large studio apartment. It was furnished with burgundy plush couches, blackout curtains, naked statues, and oil prints of devil figures—like some strange sex boudoir but missing the whips and restraints.

An earthy, salty smell wafted from a steel tub in the center—something she'd seen in fields outside of town for watering cows but with brown stuff in it, not water.

That's why this guy had flakes of mud peeling off him.

Her stomach flipped, and anxiety buzzed behind her eyes. She'd seen some strange things in her life, but this was a bit much. Taking a step backward, she decided to beg for her job back at the Kroger

The door had swung shut behind her, and before she could yank it open, the man sat up.

He rubbed his bald head and gave her a disarming grin. "I'm Jonathan; you here for the job?"

His beady black eyes met her panicked ones.

Don't leave. Stay. No need to be worried.

A little voice, one she'd never heard before, echoed in her

brain. A wave of calm washed over her. Her shoulders dropped. This was better than the Mary Jane weed she and Doug liked to share.

The half-naked man thrust a hand at Lucy, wet mud caked to his palms. She wrinkled her nose.

She ignored his chubby fingers, crossing her arms over her chest. "I'm Lucy. Lucy Lloyd."

"Well, Lucy Lloyd, come on, help me up." Jonathan waggled his fingers at her.

This time, Lucy reached down, braced her back, and hauled on one arm. Mud chunks fell to the tile as Jonathan staggered to his feet.

He rearranged his little Speedo. "Thanks, you're stronger than you look for an old biddy."

Lucy resisted the urge to slap him. Old biddy, her eye. What, did he think he was an Adonis?

She pointed to the water trough. "Why do you have that in your living room?"

Jonathan limped down the short hall, the oil lamps casting odd shadows on his back. "I do like myself a Moorish mud bath. Follow me."

Lucy slipped off her shoes and left them at the door. She padded down the hall in her bare feet. The warm smell of the mud was soothing, and she could hear a few strains of opera playing softly from a Victrola turntable on an ornate wood end table.

A sense of ease and lethargy trickled through her veins.

"What kind of companion are you looking for?" Lucy stuck one finger into the warm mud.

With a lurch, Jonathan grabbed her and tossed her head-first into the tub.

Fire hot alarm blazed through her nervous system, and she fought to right herself. A thick, viscous fluid filled her mouth, and she was stuck like an ant in molasses. Panic clenched her chest. How could she be so stupid? The guy was a serial killer, a pervert, she was going to die—

Jonathan grabbed her arms and pulled her head out of the mud. His brows were pulled together, and fury blazed out of his eyes.

"I can smell that you are not AB negative. You are definitely ordinary O. That will not do."

Lucy tried to fight him, but the sludge held her arms. She was a wolf in a trap. She fought but was exhausting herself. Forcing herself to settle, she tried to think. When you were born as poor as she was, you had to use your brain to survive.

Jonathan took a deep breath, and contemplation replaced anger as he blinked. "Maybe you can help me find some AB. My knees just aren't what they used to be."

Lucy coughed, and brown chunks flew out of her mouth. She took a deep, ragged breath. "Why do you care what my blood type is?"

Maybe she would live to see tomorrow if she played this right. A sprinkle of hope washed away some of her terror.

Jonathan ignored her question. "It won't take the leeches long; let them do their thing. It's easier that way."

A huge shiver shook her entire body despite the warm mud. "What do you mean leeches?"

He pushed her head back under the sludge, and then she felt them. The mud was moving. Wiggling. The mud was full of thousands of leeches. They were on her. Sticking to her skin, her cheeks, in her hair ...

If the veiny hands of Doug made her nauseous, that was nothing compared to this horror. The slugs were slimy, slippery, and oozing all over her. She was a living chocolate lava cake. She was light-headed. From blood loss? From sensory overload? She tried to scream, the leeches squiggling into her mouth, choking her—clogging her airway—

When Lucy's eyes fluttered open, she leaped up, her hands frantically tearing at her skin. There was nothing there. She was showered and dressed in a black catsuit.

Did she own a black catsuit? NO. The way it hung off her skinny hips, she knew it wasn't flattering. But now wasn't the time to stress about fashion.

Her stomach flipped as if the thousands of leeches were squirming inside of her. Her shaking hands scrubbed her legs and arms. A frantic look around showed not a leech to be seen. Had she imagined the whole thing? The mud-filled tub was still in the middle of the room, but the top was still, thick, and impenetrable. No leeches.

She sat back down on the burgundy leather couch, dizzy. Once her heart stopped pounding, she realized something.

She felt amazing.

Young and vital.

She knew she had come here for a job but couldn't remember much else. She looked at her hands. There were tiny slits in her hands.

What?

She looked closer at her palms, but then a heavy-set man with bulldog features in a fancy suit walked in from the next room.

Jonathan. He'd changed out of his hideous bathing suit.

She'd answered an ad in the paper.

Her eyes popped and her blood ran cold as she remembered

He pushed her into the tub! There were leeches!

Lucy slowed her breathing, eyes darting for an escape, a way out of this gothic basement hellhole. Jonathan raised his arms to calm her, his black tuxedo riding up to his elbows, his black beady eyes on her like a dog coveting a steak bone.

"If you touched me ..." she said, baring her teeth.

A horrified expression crossed his face. "I would never! I am a gentleman."

Lucy snorted. She'd met lots of so-called gentlemen.

She flexed her fingers. No arthritis. God, she felt good. There were two sore spots in the middle of her palms, but that was it. Maybe she could fight him?

"Jonathan, you have some explaining to do." His amused smirk infuriated her. "Before I call the fuzz."

He put his chubby hands up in protest. "I promise, nothing of the sort. You had a bath and were so relaxed you fell asleep. In my special Moorish mud."

She snorted and pointed a remarkably youthful-looking finger at him. "Right, buddy. I don't know what kind of kinky game you got going on, but I'm out of here."

"No game, no kink." The smirk still on his face.

Lucy stood up and made a fist, prepared to punch him in the gut if she had to. The silky glide of the bodysuit reminded her she wasn't wearing her own clothes.

"Where's my stuff, you pervert?"

"Let me plead my case. Maybe I should have done this before your mud bath." Jonathan twirled his bowtie. "Don't you deserve to make some easy money?"

Lucy unballed her fists. "I'm listening."

"Look, first things first. I'll pay you 50 cents an hour to be my companion, but I can't hunt anymore. I've become a tad portly." He gestured down at his belly, slivers of skin pushing through his white button-down shirt. "I need you to be my Renfield."

Lucy jerked as realization flooded her. She'd recently seen the premiere of *Dracula* at the drive-in with Doug.

"Why do you need a Renfield?" she said slowly, thinking there was no way this ugly guy was a vampire.

He smiled. "It's easy money, Lucy."

How many times had the lure of easy money gotten her into trouble?

She took a deep breath. "I definitely need some cash for rent."

Jonathan smiled, and his eyes flickered with a weird light.

Lucy felt woozy and comfortable again, like she had when she first arrived tonight.

He talked and she listened. But she couldn't recall the conversation—

Next thing she knew, she was out on the sidewalk, the moon bathing her in an eerie light. The cool air tossed her fresh, sleek hair—no more split ends; no bleach fried curls.

Lucy now had a mission.

Bring Jonathan back someone with AB negative blood.

Flickers of memory tickled her brain. He'd given her a vial of blood to sniff. Her taste buds salivated as she recalled taking a small taste (*Delicious*). Her disappointment when he wouldn't let her have more. The promise that she could have a whole cup when she came back with prey. Someone with the right blood type.

She jogged down the sidewalk, feeling better than she had in years. She could smell the top pinecone in that tall tree. She took a deep breath of the feral odor of a raccoon hiding under the park bench.

Lucy had never felt this ... powerful. So why was she running errands for a man?

Right. She needed the money because damn Doug left her.

If she needed a victim, she knew the perfect place to hunt. In minutes, she was at the cemetery and crouched behind a gravestone. She'd never stalked anyone before, but this felt natural. Hunching on the grass, she could see in the dark like a cat. She shivered in happiness.

The sore spots on her palms opened and closed. There were little mouths in her palms—that's what those slits were. She gasped but then shrugged.

She felt younger, could see in the dark, and had super smell. Who cared if she had little jaws in her hands?

Each was the size of a dime and had crowded rows of sharp teeth. They gnashed and kissed. The sound was subtle, like a baby grasping at a bottle. She shuddered. She'd never wanted to be a housewife OR a mother.

All of this felt cosmically correct somehow. It reminded her of how she felt every time she met a new potential boyfriend. Perfect. It was fate. This was what the universe wanted for her.

Thinking of boyfriends, if her slimy ex-sugar daddy was telling the truth, Doug should be showing up any minute. He'd be here or at the Bingo Hall. She furrowed her brows. What did he see in Vera—?

And there he was. A shiver of delight ran up her spine.

Doug staggered down the manicured path, half drunk. His jeans sagged down over the crack of his butt, and his hair was stuck to his head in a greasy gray comb over.

Rather than flowers, he pulled some mushrooms out of a brown paper bag and placed them in front of a small tombstone about ten feet from where Lucy hid. Then he pulled out a bottle of Schlitz beer and took several long swallows.

"Elizabeth, you old bitch, you got what you deserved." He poured the last of his drink over her stone.

Lucy used her newly-sharp night vision and read the inscription on the gravestone.

Elizabeth Doober, wife of Doug Doober. She always said her feet were killing her, but I didn't believe her. 1898-1958.

Lucy bit her lip. That lying asshole. He wasn't having

problems getting over his dead wife. The dirty old man had just been using her for cheap sex and easy company. Lucy sniffed the air; was Doug AB negative? She shook her head. He smelt more A positive.

Doug pulled down his pants and peed on Elizabeth's grave. The sound of splashing made Lucy cringe. Despicable. How could she have let those gross hands touch her body?

The little mouths on her hands growled. She was hungry. Weird to feel hunger pangs that started in her belly and laced up to her hands like mini bolts of electricity.

Doug's blood would be diluted with cheap beer but a fine old vintage nonetheless. She salivated, like when she poured her first glass of Dubonnet wine every day. Perhaps she could take a tiny taste and then take him back to Jonathan? It's not like he'd given her hard and fast rules for this new job.

A shudder of anticipation shook her sinewy frame.

Lucy crept up behind Doug and positioned herself behind the adjacent tombstone. The man was still watering his wife's grave. A super-sized bladder for an old guy. She hesitated. No matter how foul, he was still human. Plus, they did have a few good times together.

Spending his money in the town's best pub.

Drinking coffee on his porch, waiting to make sure the garbage truck took every bag.

A smile touched her lips; she loved cat-calling the garbage boys. Doug would whistle right along with her, slapping his thigh and grading bag tossing techniques.

Some good times with Mr. Doug Doober. Maybe she should find a victim she didn't know?

She hesitated, but when Doug started singing and doing a strange dance while shaking off the final drops of urine—

She pounced.

Landing on his back like a hungry leech, she laid one hand on his neck and the other on the wrist that lunged up at her.

"What the hell?" He staggered backward and tripped over his ankle-puddled pants.

Lucy rode him like a bull rider to the ground. The little suction pads in her one palm latched on to his carotid artery, and the other, the major vein in his wrist. He rolled in the damp grass, pulling at her with his one free arm.

'Yeehaw." Lucy moaned as the refreshing, delicious fluid spread up her arms and into her circulatory system.

"Liz? You back from the dead?" he squeaked, his face smashed into the ground.

Lucy had secreted a bit of sedative and painkiller through her palms so her latching was unnoticeable. She knew this intuitively. As she knew leeches used hirudin to thin blood.

As his struggling slowed, Lucy kissed him on the cheek. Her eyes rolled back as refreshment and rejuvenation flowed through her body.

Doug was done.

Lucy stopped sucking as soon as he passed out. Jittering her hands to release the suction pods, she fell onto to the grass, satiated.

"Dang, Jonathan isn't going to like you draining his dinner," she said to herself, looking up at the night stars. Then she shrugged. Since when did she care what other people liked?

Putting one finger to Doug's neck, she checked for a pulse. Yes, there was still one there. He hadn't died; she'd stopped in time. The old asshole would wake up with a few hickeys, feeling weak and disoriented. He would probably dismiss the whole thing as a dream. Lucy hoped Liz did star in his nightmare. Maybe he would bring her flowers instead of mushrooms and piss next time.

She stretched, fluffing up her thick, healthy hair. Best to get out of there before Doug recovered. She needed to find a new victim; hopefully, AB negative, for Jonathan.

She felt fantastic, her cheeks glowing pink, her legs like a maiden racehorse.

Putting her hands to her cheeks (the little mouths quiet and almost invisible now), she could feel the flesh plump and moist. She felt like a 20-year-old again.

Using her new spurt of energy, Lucy loped back into town. Some sexy Elvis Presley music leaked out of the local pub, and she stopped to enjoy the music. There might be some young, hot stud with AB negative blood in there enjoying a cocktail.

Her stomach flipped as she thought of young, virile men. Like the muscular garbage man she ogled from Doug's porch. She ran her hands over her spandex outfit. Her body felt taut and able.

"Rrrrrr," she growled. "This leech lady is hungry."

The flickering of the neon bar sign called to her. But she better get some dinner for her new boss. Work first, play later.

She wiggled her arthritis-free fingers. Lord, she felt strong. She clenched her fists, the nails tickling the satiated little mouths, quiet for now.

Why did she need a man in her life anyways? Why should she work for Jonathan?

Bring Jonathan back someone with AB negative blood.

She shook off the subliminal command. She clenched her hungry palms. Jonathan had obviously tried some mumbo jumbo leech mind-melding with her.

Lucy hadn't listened to her parents, her teachers, or her boss at the Kroger. Why should she start listening to anyone else now?

Jonathan was fat and out of shape. She could take him if he gave her any trouble. He'd been knocked down by a door, for crying out loud.

Why should she work for him?

All she wanted was an easy life. With her new powers, she

might be on to something. What did a lady need anyways? Not a sugar daddy, that's for sure.

A few bucks to buy nice dresses.

A tub full of mud.

Some warm blood on a Friday night.

A hot young garbage man.

She smiled to herself and pushed her way into the pub. The stale air, throbbing rock music, and aroma of different blood types were intoxicating.

Lucy did deserve the finer things in life. And she was going to take them.

Wishbone

By Candace Nola

Judith Stenson huffed as she heaved the turkey onto the counter. The puff of air pushed the loose hair from her eye and freed the droplet of sweat from the tip of her nose. Jim had brought home a heavy one this year, every damn year in fact. Goddamn thirty-pound bird for ten people. He acted like they were hosting the dinner party of the year when, in reality, it was his uppity parents, his frigid snob of a sister, Tilly, and her aunt Marge and uncle Stewart. His boss, Dale, along with his wife and their baby, would round out the feast this year.

She snorted and grabbed a bottle of coke from the icebox. Behind her, rows of pies, a pound cake, and loaves of bread and rolls cooled on the table. The baby was the only person she was currently looking forward to seeing. Jim's boss had married a younger woman, and she had a baby last winter. Billy was adorable, with his dark hair and gray eyes, plump cheeks and chubby legs. He was almost as hefty as the damn turkey.

She sighed as she freed the turkey from its wrappings,

setting the gizzards aside for later use. Well, if nothing else, she mused, she could relieve the young woman of the baby for the day and spend time spoiling him in the kitchen while the rest of them criticized her cooking, sniffed their wine through haughty nostrils, and droned about the state of the world. She was all for letting it burn.

Foolishness is what it was. Judith was tired, sick and tired. After fifteen years of marriage, the light had left her eyes and her heart had grown cold. This was not what she had envisioned as a little girl playing dress-up in her mother's wedding gown and high heels. This was soul-crushing, demeaning, joyless free labor chained to a man she had grown to loathe. Jim had been kind once, or so she thought, kind just long enough to pull the wool over her eyes and that of her mother's.

She had been smitten by the dashing young man with the piercing green eyes the moment she saw him. Her mother needed to buy a new car, and Judith went with her and her Uncle Stewart to look around at the local car lot. Jim had been new, both on the job and in town. Judith spent half the time trying not to blush every time he locked eyes with her. She trailed along behind Uncle Stewart as he kicked tires and haggled with Jim's boss about the price.

An hour later, after one ice-cold Coca-Cola clumsily handed to her by Jim as her mother signed the papers with Uncle Stewart, and Judith had officially been asked on a date. She rode home in the new car, blushing and giggling with her mother, not even caring about the soft leather seats she sat on or the shiny new interior of the car.

After her father passed away, things slowly fell into disrepair as repairmen refused to come to the home without a man present. Her mother spent many afternoons frustrated and angry, trying to paint the fences that lined their neat lawn, trim the hedges in the front yard, and maintain everything by herself. Her pride did not allow her to beg, and she turned away the neighbor's son several times, not wishing for nor wanting the charity. Soon after, her uncle moved his family closer to them so he could help his sister more.

Judith found it ridiculous that her mother needed a chaperone to go buy a car, but she was with her when she had tried to go to two different car lots and was turned away. Once by an overweight greaseball of an owner, chiding her for coming to talk "man business" without a man. When informed of her husband's passing, the man tutted to her like she was a child and told her to come back with her father then. Judith never forgot the way her mother had turned on her heel, lips tight in a slim line, and strode away, holding her head high. The second lot had been kinder in their rejection of her, but still, no man, no car.

Judith had been infuriated, but her mother reminded her that they had to know their place in the world. Men ruled the world. It was just how it was. Mary Ann Stenson did not plan on her husband dying, nor did she plan on her widow status being ignored, with those in charge still requiring her to have a man everywhere she went, except the grocer's, of course, and the hairdresser's. And here, years later, things were still the same, except with Judith in her mother's shoes.

Her mom had passed away almost five years ago, and Judith still felt the ache in her heart like it was yesterday. A sheen of tears filled her eyes as she reached for the faucet to run cold water over the defrosting carcass in her sink. She sniffed, refusing to let the tears fall. She reached for her chopping knife instead, choosing to take out her anger on the potatoes and onions. Knife in hand, vegetables at her mercy, she began to slice and dice in preparation for tomorrow's dinner. The heat in the kitchen had nothing on the anger boiling in her veins.

Two hours later, Judith heard the front door slam. Her head drooped for a moment before she shook herself and admonished her reflection to snap out of it. She ignored the strands of hair that filled the sink, purposefully refusing to acknowledge the speed with which she was losing her curls.

"Could be worse, you know," she hissed into the mirror. "I could be a spinster with nothing to my name." Her dark eyes gleamed in the bright light. Internally, her sarcastic voice told her that may be preferable over her current state of affairs, reminding her that she already *had* nothing, would be nothing except the property of her husband or, worse, shunned by society for not being shackled to a man.

Judith squeezed the bridge of her nose, smoothed the skirt of her dress, freshly donned, and forced a smile on her newly made-up and powdered face.

"Judy, I'm home!" Jim yelled up the stairs. "Bring me a beer."

She grimaced as his voice entered her ears like shards of glass against a tin roof. The anger boiled in her gut, and she took a breath to steady herself.

"Coming, dear," she called, pleasantly as she could, swallowing the bile back down into her gut, where it burned and churned within her, toxic acid eating a hole through her insides. She could feel it, bit by bit, being chewed away like the rest of her.

Her heels clacked on the freshly mopped stairs as she glided down them to wait on her husband for the evening. His every beck and call were hers to fulfill. She went into the kitchen first and stared at the counters full of baked goods for the holiday. Bottles of wine, carefully selected, stood nearby to be chilled. The oven was warming Jim's dinner, and the refrigerator was stuffed full of carefully prepared dishes waiting to be baked in the morning.

She pulled a beer out, popped the top off, and entered the

living room, where Jim had already settled into his easy chair. He took it from her, then looked at her expectantly.

"Well?" he asked.

"How was your day, dear?" Judith said, smiling down at his ruddy face. He was always sweaty these days. Time hadn't been kind to him, and his gut hung over his belt a tad more than before.

"Not that." He glowered. "My shoes, did you forget your duties? My god, I've been at work all day. Do I really need to come home to tell you what to do too? What have you done all day, anyway? The house is filthy, and it's hot in here, too hot." He mopped his brow with a handkerchief and slurped at his beer.

He grinned when she bent down to remove his shoes. With a swift jerk, he kicked upwards, stopping just short of kicking her in the face. She flinched, stepping back suddenly from the motion. She glared at him, biting her tongue so hard it bled.

"Next time, I won't stop. Now stop being a lazy cow and fetch my slippers," he demanded.

When she started toward the closet for his slippers, his voice stopped her in her tracks.

"Shoes. First. Then my slippers. Are you even listening?" His voice was cold and cruel as he spat the words at her, then flung the empty beer bottle at her feet. "Hurry up, damnit. I'm starving."

"Yes, dear. Sorry, dear," she uttered, breathing deeply through her nose before she could say anything else.

She stepped over to him, bent low, and removed his shoes. Then she handed him the newspaper. After he took it, she went to get his slippers, smiling like a frozen mannequin the entire time. She put them on, refusing to acknowledge the stench drifting from his swollen feet. He didn't even look up from the paper as she finished.

"Beer. And I'll eat in here," Jim ordered as she straightened. He gave her a dismissive wave, and she left the room, keeping her steps light as her burden grew heavier.

In the kitchen, she went to the oven, opened it, and bent low to retrieve the pot roast, ignoring the searing pain in her back. It had been excruciating for days, but there was no point in telling Jim. Doctors were expensive, and Jim wasn't going to waste money on one only to find out it was just her "womanly things" causing her discomfort. The first visit had given grave news only for Jim to leave in a huff, embarrassed that her doctor was speaking of such things.

"All part of being of a woman," he used to sneer when she tried to tell him about the pain she experienced, monthly cycle or not.

"Get over it. You sit on your ass all day and do nothing while I work and have the nerve to complain? You're just ungrateful. Your mother should have taught you better manners." He would storm from the room, not even bothering to help her up from the floor where she had fallen.

She let out a muffled whimper when she straightened with the heavy tray in her hands, barely able to set it on the stovetop before the pain surged down her hips and into her leg. She took a deep breath, reaching behind her with both hands to gently massage the burning spot in her spine. Inhale. Exhale. Slowly, the pain eased, and she began to prepare Jim's plate.

The meat was tender and falling apart. The vegetables were crisp and perfectly roasted. She added two thick slices of fresh bread to the side of his tray and placed two more bottles of beer next to them. Hopefully, he'd eat and fall asleep in his chair again. She lifted the tray and carried it out to him.

Jim barely glanced at her as she set the tray down next to him and quietly left the room.

"You better be serving something better than this slop for tomorrow," he called after her. She flinched as the words hit her ears, each one cutting deeper than the last. He hadn't had time to take a bite, but yet he was insulting her anyway.

She almost snorted, glad he wasn't in earshot. She quietly cleared her throat and went into the kitchen to eat her dinner alone. Jim hadn't left a morsel on his plate in fifteen years. He just bitched to hear his own voice. She almost pitied him, almost. But he had used up all her goodwill years ago. His boss was more of a narcissistic ass than even Jim was. It couldn't be easy for him, working for a man like that, constantly belittling him, putting him down; but oh wait, why was that so familiar to her?

She snorted again and prepared her own plate, poured a glass of red wine, and sat down in the quiet kitchen, surrounded by her day's labor. She ate slowly, taking in the solitude of the kitchen, a place she could almost claim as her own. Jim rarely came in here for anything, declaring the kitchen a woman's place and it was her duty to fetch and carry anything he might need.

On the rare occasion that Jim wanted to invite his boss over or his old friends from school, he would swagger around the house like the biggest rooster in the barnyard, cocky and jubilant. Bragging and crowing over his house, his wife, his shiny car outside, his few precious treasures that were really artifacts from a war he had never been in, things passed down from his grandpa.

On those nights, Jim loved to call her pet names and swat her on the ass as she walked by, heaping on affection and attention like he was competing for a prize. Those nights, he would play host and would enter the kitchen with her to retrieve beer and cocktails; of course, all while making sure she was fetching the appetizers.

Judith silently shook with rage, chaotic thoughts swirling through her brain as she idly pushed the remains of her meal around her plate, not even tasting the morsels she had eaten.

She lifted her glass of wine to sip from it and was surprised at the tremble in her hand. She stared at it for a moment, downed the scarlet ambrosia in a single gulp, and sent the glass flying against the wall.

She grinned without humor as the crystal shattered, sending glistening bits of glass across the floor. Not a word came from the other room, as expected. The kitchen was her area. If she dropped it, it was up to her to clean it up. Jim wouldn't so much as wander in here to see if she had keeled over from a heart attack, at least not until he needed a beer and she didn't answer his demand. Even then, it would be beer first, then gazing at her limp body on the floor, trying to decide if he should call for help or if it was her *womanly troubles* out to embarrass him again.

She snickered. The next time her period hit, she should skip the bulky pad and underthings. Just let the blood flow down her legs, splatter on the floors and the carpeting and the new velvet sofa. Leave the toilet full of red clotted water, and the shower smeared with dark crimson stains.

The next time he demanded sex from her during her cycle, she should let him have it, skip telling him it was that time of the month. Let him mount her without a word and then see the horror on his face as she soaked him with the blood from her vacant womb. She could almost see him backpedaling away while she lay laughing on the bed, disgust on his face, quickly followed by rage. His gut wobbling over his dick, boxers around his ankles as she lay there laughing, eager and hungry for what came next.

She would welcome the blows. She would allow it, hit after hit, marking her face, bruising her flesh. She would laugh and laugh as each hit came. Her voice coming in breathy laughs, equal part pain and hysteria, egging him on as he pummeled her, until finally, blissfully, darkness would come for her soul, then freedom.

"Judith!" Jim's angry demand came from the living room, snapping her out of her daydream. He must have called more than once. She rose stiffly and walked slowly into the other room.

"Yes, dear," she said, standing at his side as he glared at her.

"Where were you? I called for you three times."

"In the powder room, dear. I must not have heard you."

"You disgust me. I don't need to hear such things," he sneered, looking her up and down, disgust in his eyes. "Take this away and bring me another beer." He waved a single hand in her direction. Dismissed.

Judith stared at him for a long moment, feeling her jaw clench beneath the mannequin smile. The roar of rushing blood, an ocean of pulsing white noise, filled her ears, her skull, her brain. Her heart thudded ever harder against her ribs. She breathed. Inhale. Exhale. She lifted the tray and turned back toward the kitchen, heels clicking smartly across the floor as the pearls around her neck inched closer to choking her delicate throat.

━━

Judith lay in bed that night staring at the ceiling, lost in thought. Every sound made her blood run cold. She held her breath with every creak and groan, every whisper of the tree branches outside her window scratching across the windowpane. Jim had not come upstairs yet. She hoped he would stay down there, snoring away in his chair like an overgrown slug.

Tears of frustration threatened to spill from her dark eyes, but she refused to let them come. Fifteen long years of frustration, anger, and hurt pulsed in her body like waves crashing on the shore, breaking and breaking and breaking. Judith was bone-deep weary, but more so, she was changing. She could feel it. A ticking bomb nestled in her chest, flame already ignited. She both welcomed and dreaded what would happen when the timer ran out.

This was not how she saw her life playing out. The memories of a happier time surfaced and played across the ceiling above her like a picture show. Her mother and father waltzing in the living room. The pure love in their eyes when they looked at one another. The small touches when they passed one another. The respect in their voices when they spoke. The adoration they showered upon her.

Holidays had been wonderful times, full of warm kitchens and baked goods, roaring fires and Christmas tales told by the adults with cocktails in hand. She remembered being perched on the steps, hot cocoa in hand as she listened to the grown-ups tell stories from their past and her father told off-color jokes that made her mother and Aunt Margaret blush and giggle. She remembered how much her father had adored her, how protected she felt when he was nearby, how kind he had been.

Judith had been so sheltered, so protected from the reality of this life, that she had been blindsided when her father passed away. Seeing the new way of life her mother had to endure, being without a husband or father to handle her affairs, the indignity of it all. The condescending tone of their voices. No one had treated them this way when her father was alive. Life turned cold and quiet then.

Barely sixteen, Judith did not quite understand why everyone was suddenly so strange, why people they knew were suddenly so cold and cruel. Why her college-educated mother was being treated like an uneducated pauper. Until finally, Mary Ann sat her daughter down and explained the world to her. Things that Judith thought she knew became much clearer than ever before. The nuances of her life that had surrounded her snapped into place with a resounding click that reverberated within her for months after.

Her mother had explained things to her and ended her lecture with the best advice she could give her daughter. Find a good, kind man like your father and always, always save the pin money for a rainy day in case you don't. "Pin money", she had called it. Judith still found the term funny, though she knew what it meant. Mary Ann religiously saved all the spare money she could from the grocer's, the milkman, the butcher's, taking in washing from their neighbors and sewing too. Coffee cans full of bills and loose coins that she stashed away in high cabinets.

Judith had asked her once why she did it, and Mary Ann had simply replied it was her pin money, kept for a rainy day, then handed Judith two quarters to spend at the candy store on the corner. Two quarters taken right from that old coffee can on the top shelf behind the flour. She had never forgotten it, and in those lean years after her father passed on, her mother's pin money bought their milk and groceries for quite a while.

Judith had kept the tradition after her marriage, saving what she could, however she could. She did the washing and ironing for old Mrs. Esther next door, and the widower, Mr. Jones, down the block too. She learned how to use coupons for groceries, saving pennies and dimes on cuts of meat and loaves of bread. Jim never questioned her when she paid the milkman or did the shopping, and he never held his hand out for change, expecting her to have spent the allowed amount on food to keep him fat and happy, or at least fat as time went on.

It all went into her stash. Kept with her lady things and behind the baking supplies and lined up behind the washing powder in the laundry room. Old tin cans full of change. Judith figured that maybe her rainy day was coming and maybe *that change* rattling around those old cans signified *her change*. A change that was long overdue.

Judith nodded to herself. There in the dark, she made

peace with doing what must be done, if she survived. She lay there until morning, staring into the shadows, seeing nothing but her mother's kind face looking back. She didn't stir until dawn peeked in her window. Judith rose, resolved to get through Thanksgiving dinner the best she could, and then she would take things from there.

Judith filled the sink with warm water for the dishes so she could clean as she cooked. Breakfast for Jim sizzled on the stovetop while his snores still echoed from the living room. She wouldn't bother waking him and risk his wrath so early in the morning. It was *his* day off and time for *him* to relax and enjoy himself. She pressed her ruby-painted lips into a thin line and tried to clear the intrusive thoughts from her mind. *Not today, just please, not today.*

Today, she had to perform for Jim's horse and pony show and prance around like the perfect housewife. Tomorrow, she could be angry and alone and stew in a rage. Right now, she had to cook. She flipped the bacon over in the pan, wincing as the grease popped along her hands. Then she dumped the bowl of peppers and onions in the eggs and briskly stirred those so they wouldn't burn. The bubbling of the coffee percolating on the opposite counter calmed her nerves as the scent of the fresh brew filled the room. She inhaled deeply, pausing for a moment to soak in the aroma as well as the silence.

Judith let out a deep sigh, feeling the shift in her bones as a weight released from her. She savored the moment, not caring just then that it was only a brief respite. Just then, she was grateful to have it. She turned to the refrigerator and heaved the massive roasting pan from the bottom shelf. Pain ran up her spine as she straightened, and she was momentarily overcome. Nausea and a clammy sweat followed. Judith refused to cry out. She slowly maneuvered herself to an upright position with the heavy tray and set it down on the counter.

She counted to ten, breathing heavily, willing the pain to subside. Tears glazed her eyes, and she blinked, swiping them away with the back of her hand. The pearl necklace swayed gently as she rubbed at her face, and she idly brought her other hand up to clutch the pearls tightly against her bosom. The string of pearls had been given to her when her mother had passed, those and her wedding ring, both of which Judith wore daily.

Her mother's gold band sat flush against her own. Those two items were all she had left of her parents. Her father had bought both for her mother many years ago, and now they were gone, nothing left but a string of pearls, a gold band, and a wave of memories that still tugged at her hurt and broken places like nothing else could.

Gingerly, she lifted the pan once more and set it into the waiting oven. As she closed the oven door, she heard Jim clomping over to the stairs. She said a silent prayer that he went up them and did not enter the kitchen yet. His heavy footsteps began to trudge up the staircase, and she turned back to the counter. There, she began slicing fruit for breakfast and for the fruit salad for after dinner. She worked quietly, listening for Jim to make his way down the stairs again, demanding to be fed. Judith finished the fruit bowl and had set it aside when his heavy steps echoed in the hallway.

Judith grabbed a plate and put his breakfast on it. Eggs, bacon, potatoes, toast, all on one plate. Freshly sliced fruit went into a bowl, followed by his coffee and juice. She poured coffee for herself and took a sip of it before carrying the tray to the dining room for Jim. She set it down at the head of the table only a moment before he entered the room.

"Bout time," he grumbled, not even glancing at her. His

tone dared her to argue. She said nothing, only waited for the dismissal.

"What the hell is this?" He growled, his heavy jowls red from the hot shower and his shave. "I don't eat this shit." He flung the bowl of fruit across the table.

"Yes, dear. I just thought you might like a bit of fruit this morning, since it's a holiday and all."

"You thought?" He finally looked at her, his expression one of feigned shock, his tone mocking. "Since when do you think?" He sneered, his lip twisting into a cruel grimace. "Clean this shit up and go cook. Dinner better be exceptional; do you hear me? None of your usual drivel. All I need is you embarrassing me in front of Dale."

Judith turned on her heel and clacked away, pearls swaying to match her hips, lips pressed closed to hide the fury. A searing blast of pain shuddered through her core, and she welcomed it then, letting it warm her boiling blood further.

━━━

By mid-afternoon, Jim was well on his way to becoming less than sober. All their guests had arrived except for Judith's aunt Marge and uncle Stewart. Dale and Jim laughed loud and hard in the den, smoke filling the room from their cigars. Liquor was consumed in large amounts as Jim called for Judith, over and over, insisting that she serve them. Jim laughed uproariously every time Dale swatted Judith on the ass when she passed by.

Twice, he lingered there, rubbing the curve of her bottom as she poured his drink. Jim just grinned, rocking back on his heels, but the dark glint in his eye said more than words ever could. *Don't you dare embarrass me.* The threat was silent but there as he watched her flinch away from Dale's exploring hands. She quickly covered it by excusing herself to serve the ladies in the other room and gave both Dale and Jim a tight but polite smile as she left the room.

Grace sat quietly on the sofa in the living room, Billy on her lap, while Jim's sister, Tilly, perched at the other end, glaring at everything and everyone. Judith had set trays of fruit and cheese in each room, along with dishes of mixed nuts, candies, and cookies. The ladies had their Sloe Gins; the men with their vodka martinis. The house smelled of turkey, tart cranberries, spiced cider, and pumpkin pie. Judith stayed on her feet, swishing from room to room, serving drinks, laughing politely when expected to, carrying trays of appetizers to the men and back again as she put the finishing touches on dinner.

By the time her aunt and uncle showed up, the table was set, the turkey was done, and everyone was filing into the dining room to be seated. Judith had laid out quite the spread. Every surface was covered with trays of food. The bar cart stood nearby with chilled wine and ice. The buffet was laden with more desserts than was necessary for ten people, but Jim had insisted on all of his favorites, of which there were many.

Judith smiled her plastic smile, greeted everyone as they entered, hung up coats, took the baby from a weary-looking Grace, and waited at her place for Jim to say grace over the meal and make a display over carving turkey. She smiled and preened and praised him like a child going potty for the first time, and he ate it up. Dale and he grinned like fools as he crowed about his prowess in carving up a dead bird. She wanted to carve him up instead. Her blood boiled in her veins as Tilly poked at every dish, sniffing haughtily at each item and declaring it *not as good as her mother's, but it'll do.*

"Don't be offended, Judith dear. It is nice that you tried to make our mother's recipe, but maybe you could just ask her next time." Tilly tittered, smirking at her mother across from her. "I mean, she is right here. It's not like she wasn't invited. I'm sure Mother would have loved to help you."

"Of course, how silly of me." Judith tittered, full plastic smile firmly in place. "I'll be sure to ask next time."

"Please do, dear. It's so sad that your mother passed away before she could properly teach you the basics," Trudy added in, peering down her nose at Judith. Her husband, Bert, nodded beside her, patting her hand.

"So kind of you, dear," he praised her, beaming at Judith. "Isn't she so kind?"

"Thank you so much for the offer," Judith said tightly. Unable to bear any more, she rose with the baby in her arms and took him to the kitchen under the pretense of feeding him. She felt the flush in her cheeks and knew her neck and bosom would be deep crimson with anger.

"How dare they?" she fumed quietly in the kitchen, talking to the drooling baby as he cooed at her. "I made *my mother's* recipes, not that daft old woman's, the absolute fools," she muttered, seething, grinding her teeth until her jaw ached.

She sat calmly for a moment, then started feeding the baby the mashed potatoes she had set aside for him. He giggled and babbled as she held him, bouncing him slightly on her knee in between bites. Snatches of the dinner conversation drifted to her ears as Billy ate, and anger grew dangerously loud in her heart, blooming like burst blood vessels, rippling into throbbing veins, boiling her bones, incinerating her very marrow. In the kitchen, Billy fed while something inside Judith changed.

━━━

Judith reappeared in the dining room, holding a full carafe of steaming spiked cider, a broad grin on her face, lips plump and rosy from newly applied lipstick. Billy cooed from the kitchen, safe in the playpen Grace had set up for him. Nine less than sober faces looked at her. A mix of humor, disdain, and hostility greeted her.

"Who's ready for cider?" she cheerily declared. "I've got the spice cake freshly iced, still warm, and there're all kinds of goodies just over there on the buffet."

Judith went from person to person, pouring the cider into the glass mugs she had set out. Jim eyed her warily but kept his own smile glued to his face as Judith shot him a wink, then began serving desserts from her mother's favorite tray. A slight flush clung to her skin, a fine sheen of sweat coated her upper lip and clung to the small of her back as every step she took sent lava through her veins.

She hid the pain, kept smiling and serving her guests. Judith raved over the ladies' hairstyles, their fine clothes, the rings on their fingers, and praised their husbands for being such fine specimens and providers. She even grazed the back of Dale's sweaty neck with her polished fingernails, hiding her disgust as she felt the shudder of pleasure run through him. He practically leered at her as she passed him by. Jim sat and grinned and toasted.

Judith took her seat at the table and sipped her coffee, her plastic smile plastered in place. The dinner went on as the laughs grew louder and the insults deeper, even as the voices grew more slurred, like molasses oozing across a kitchen counter. Through it all, Judith smiled and nodded and laughed, patiently waiting. A woman on fire.

———

By the time dessert was over, her guests were slumped in their chairs, eyes rolling and glassy. The narcotics Judith had crushed into the cider had done a wonderful job of rendering the whole lot of them nearly paralyzed. Jim could barely keep his head up as he looked at her.

"Whass' the matter wif everyone, Judy?" he slurred. His head lolled on his shoulders, and he tried to lift it again. "Wha' did'ya do?"

"Well now, dear. I only did what every good wife should do," Judith said, smiling. "I cooked. I cleaned. I washed. I ironed. I fucked. I served. I shopped. I smiled. I did as I was told." She leaned back in her chair and gazed around at her guests. All of them struggled to focus on her.

She rose gracefully and began to walk slowly around the table, stopping behind Tilly's chair.

"I endured endless amounts of your insults, your blathering. Your drunk behavior and those of your cohorts. I have stood mute while you assaulted me, allowed your buddies to violate me, and stood by while your parents insulted my every move." Judith placed her hands on Tilly's shoulders, gripped them hard.

"And you!" she exclaimed, ripping Tilly's head backward, forcing the woman to look at her. "When I lost my babies, you dared to blame me. Not once, but twice." Judith stared at her coldly, raised one hand, and slapped Tilly hard across her face.

Tilly's head rocked back, but Judith wasn't done with her. She grabbed her hair again and forced her face down into the dredges of her dinner plate. Congealed gravy and mashed potatoes splattered as Tilly struggled to breathe. Raspy whimpers came from her, but the drug Judith had put in the cider only allowed the smallest of movements.

Judith pushed with both arms, keeping her face planted in the mess, smiling at Jim while she did so.

"You allowed this," she said to him. Venom dripped from her words as she stared at him, barely flinching from Tilly's struggles against her. "I loved you. You betrayed my love, and my trust, and that of my mother."

Tilly stopped moving, blood bubbles filling her plate, mixing with the gravy and turning the potatoes pink. Judith stepped away, wiping her hands on her skirt. Eight sets of eyes rolled around the room, trying to focus on her. Judith laughed as Dale fell sideways from his chair, trying to move away from the table.

"Leaving so soon?" Judith asked cheerily. Her heels clacked around the table, stopping beside Dale. She crouched down, pushed him onto his back, and ground a knee into his groin, grinning.

"How's that feel, sugar?" she cooed. "You finally got me to play with your dick." She ground harder against him, feeling his balls beneath her kneecap, sliding over and around each other, trapped in his boxers with no escape from her pointed knee. He groaned, one eye staring up at Jim as if begging for help. Drool leaked from his mouth as a tear streamed from his left eye.

Judith chuckled and rose to a crouch. "I think you look thirsty," she said. She stood over his near purple face and hiked her skirt up. She yanked her silk panties to the side and began to piss on Dale's face. The warm stream gushed from her as he sputtered beneath her. It splashed on his face and ran down his neck, slid into his hair and ears and stained his shirt. Muffled wet gurgles came from his throat as he tried to breathe and yell at the same time but could only weakly squirm beneath her like a maggot in the hot sun.

"Udy! Udy, you stap righ' now! Gah'damnit Udy!" Jim tried to yell at her, barely forming words as his tongue grew ever thicker in his mouth.

"Stop?" She stepped away from Dale, fixed her panties and skirt, then looked at the urine-soaked drunk on her floor. "Oh, I don't think I want to stop yet, Jim, dear," she said politely.

Judith neatly placed her dainty foot on Dale's neck, then slowly, seductively, ran it along his flesh with a smile, then lifted it and slammed the heel into his Adam's apple, crushing it. Blood spurted from the puncture as she stomped again, grinding her heel into Dale's throat.

When his struggles ceased, the dining room sounded like a funeral parlor, full of muffled cries and groans. Her drugged guests were struggling and writhing, trying to escape their seats, seeking any method of getting away, but their almost paralyzed bodies would not comply. Grace uttered a single wail as Judith slammed her face into the table, smashing the crystal wineglass with the delicate nose of the petite woman. The stem of broken glass disappeared into her eye socket, and Grace knew pain no more.

Judith smiled and stepped away from Dale. His ruined throat gushed blood across the gleaming floor. Her heels clacked and her pearls swayed as she strode around to stand by Jim's parents. She got low in his mom's face and spat on her, a twisted sneer on her face, fire in her eyes.

"And you, you pathetic excuse of a human," Judith said. "How dare you think you can judge me or my parents? You've never done a lick of work in your life. You sit there in your house with your servants and your cooks, and you act like some damn queen, looking down on everyone."

Judith reached over the table, enjoying the look of fear on Trudy's face. She picked up the carving knife from the turkey platter.

"The whole town knows you treat your help like trash and pay less than nothing. Everyone knows you framed that one poor girl for stealing just to get out of paying her. Everyone knows about that back-alley abortion she had." Judith raised an eyebrow at her and giggled.

"Oh, you thought no one knew? Bill got caught with his pants down, and you covered it up." Judith placed the knife against Trudy's throat, laughing as the old woman tried to grip her hands, tried to move her head, but it was futile.

Judith pulled her head up like she had with Tilly, gazing into Trudy's eyes. "You're not even worth toying with. Enjoy Hell, you evil bitch." She slid the knife deep and fast across Trudy's neck, watching the blood fall like a curtain from the slit in her throat. It coated Trudy's prized pearl necklace, double strands of white, and soaked her blouse.

Judith turned the knife on Bill, not even bothering to speak now. His eyes bulged and begged; feeble words tried to come from his mouth, but it was over before his brain knew it. Judith plunged the knife into his chest, yanked it clear, plunged again. Blood sprayed across the table, coated the china plates and the crystal glasses. It dripped from platters and bowls.

Judith grinned, enjoying herself for the first time in a decade as she finished her dinner guests. Her aunt and uncle were next, barely flinching as Judith made short work of them. The carving knife flashed, slicing and dicing ears and lips from their faces, flesh dropping to the table in fountains of blood. Uncle Stewart thought Judith didn't know what happened to her mother's money.

But Judith knew where his new car came from and that shiny new house they had built the year after her mother died. It was useful to be kind to the ladies around town, very useful indeed, especially the bank ladies. Judith chuckled as they bled, then slumped to the floor, their faces carved off, bone and muscle exposed.

"That'll teach you to be two-faced," she sneered. "Now we can see what you're really made of." Her aunt's eyes bulged from naked grisly sockets, her cheekbones gleaming moist crimson in the low light. Her uncle lay on his side, teeth gleaming through his hollowed-out cheeks in a skeletal grin. Only Jim was left. He sat, shaking and drooling, in his chair at the head of the table.

"'Udy! Stahp 'dis. 'Udy, pwease!" Jim wheezed and rasped,

trying to speak. His eyes grew wide, and he watched her come. Bodies lay scattered around him. Blood and body fluids tainted every surface. Judith came, dripping with scarlet, hair wild with curls that had fled their pins. Her pearls swayed. Her heels clacked daintily across the floor. She paused, searching the table for something. She reached, snagged it free of the hefty carcass on the table, and turned back to her prey.

"My name is Judith!" she screamed, fury ripping from her body in one sudden release.

Her arm lifted and plunged, lifted and plunged, over and over, until her arm would no longer rise. Blood covered her. A feral yell came from her mouth: a war cry, freedom, and hysteria rolled into one. Jim slid from her grasp, landed hard on the floor. His face was frozen, an expression of terror etched across it. The turkey wishbone firmly embedded in the side of his neck. From the kitchen, the baby cooed.

How Things Are Done Here In Harmony Heights

Christine Morgan

Wake with the alarm. Shower, shave, and dress.

Downstairs, coffee ready, newspaper standing by.

"Good morning, dear!"

And there she is, picture-perfect, not a curl out of place. Makeup flawless, smile demure. Pristine apron over pressed, pleated dress. Strand of pearls, matching earrings. Heels clicking smartly on waxed linoleum.

A brief air-kiss by the cheek, so as not to muss lipstick or leave telltale marks to be the talk of the office. The fragrant whiffs of powder, hair spray, and just a hint of perfume.

"Kids! Breakfast!"

They appear. Such a lovely family. A boy—Buddy or Buster or Bobby or Billy—and girl—Sally or Susie or Sandy or Sarah. Bright-eyed and bushy-tailed, eager for school.

Happy chatter over pancakes, bacon, orange juice, milk, and eggs.

"Oh my, look at the time!"

Lunches packed, book bags in hand, and out the door they

go. Joining a cheery tide of children skipping along the sidewalk, rushing to meet the sunshine-yellow bus.

Meanwhile, hat and briefcase and final inspection. A tie minutely straightened. A stray thread plucked from a sleeve. Another air-kiss.

"Have a nice day, dear!"

The car, backing down the driveway. Sky clear and blue, manicured lawn emerald-green, white picket fence, rosy-pink flowers nodding in the garden.

She stands on the porch, beatific, waving.

At every house throughout the neighborhood, the same scene unfolds.

It's just how things are done here in Harmony Heights.

A little slice of the American Dream. Idyllic suburbia with all the modern appliances and amenities. Televisions. Automatic ice-makers.

The bus has gone. The last car pulls away.

The wives, as one, turn from the porches and step back inside. The doors close.

A hush falls.

The hush holds but for a gentle breeze rustling the trees and the amiable twitter of birds.

Nothing moves but for uniformed milkmen and mailmen making their rounds.

Until afternoon, when the bus returns. The children disembark and scamper home to waiting plates of fresh-baked cookies—chocolate chip, oatmeal-raisin, peanut butter, molasses—and glasses brimming with cool, creamy milk.

"How was school?"

Homework and then playtime. Bikes and jump-ropes, marbles and jacks, hopscotch and kick-ball. Youthful voices, exuberant laughter.

Around five-thirty, the street fills again with cars, turning one by one into their driveways.

"Welcome home, dear; how was work?"

Briefcases set down, hats removed, easy chairs settled into. Martini, with olive or cocktail onion or a twist. Or a highball, or old-fashioned, or simple whiskey, neat or on the rocks. Music from the radio; decent music, none of that vulgar rock-and-roll business. Glenn Miller, Bing Crosby, Frank Sinatra.

"Kids! Time to wash up!"

Six o'clock sharp, at the table. Supper is served. Meatloaf, or pork chops, or chicken, or veal cutlets. Potatoes and gravy. Buttered rolls. Vegetables. The prospect of dessert to encourage cleaned plates—pie, cake, a fruity gelatin mold, ice cream.

Most evenings ...

"Have fun, dear; don't stay out too late!"

Bowling league, lodge meetings, hobby-club, poker night. Smoke and manliness, camaraderie, fellowship.

Or Little League practice, Camper Scouts, pinewood derby, hearty good-natured father/son bonding time.

Before pajamas, the brushing of teeth, and bedtime.

Monday through Friday, day after day. Weekday, workday, school day.

When the weekend rolls around, Saturday sees lawns mowed, hedges trimmed, cars washed, garages and workshops puttered in. Later, popcorn in front of the television; mustn't miss Lawrence Welk!

Sunday? Church, of course. Followed by a lavish church potluck social, followed by the weekly community association meeting to discuss local concerns. Which would then be followed by a light Sunday supper of leftovers at home and a wholesome family game night of Scrabble or Yahtzee.

And then, come Monday morning, it all starts over again.

With occasional exceptions and alterations to the schedule, to be sure ... playing bridge with this couple or that, a dinner party here, a cocktail party there, birthdays, holidays, school recitals, piling everyone into the car to take in a drive-in movie. And with plenty of planned activities to keep the kids occupied during the summertime months.

So the hush holds, the perfect houses tidy and silent and serene, as the gentle breeze rustles the trees and birds amiably twitter. No dogs bark. No cats prowl. No babies cry. The uniformed milkmen and mailmen pass like phantoms, dropping off their deliveries, not so much as acknowledging one another should their paths happen to cross. No sales-people, census-takers, or opinion-pollsters knock upon a single door.

Because that's just how things are done here in Harmony Heights.

"Gentlemen? Gentlemen!" Frank Ashton raised his voice, competing with the rolling rumble and crash of pins echoing throughout Harmony Lanes.

Nearby conversations quelled. Men in bowling shirts sporting their various team logos turned toward him.

"Before we begin," he went on, once he had their attention, "I'd like you all to join me in congratulating our own Walter Grady on his new promotion!"

He gestured expansively with his cigar-hand, causing a whorl of smoke, at the aforementioned Walter, who awkwardly cleared his throat as everyone broke out in clapping and cheers.

"Aw, shucks, fellas," Walter said. "It's not official; I haven't accepted yet."

"Pffff, details" Frank smacked him on the back hard enough to stagger him. "It's as good as yours!"

"Haven't accepted yet?" scoffed John Parker. "Why in the world not?"

"I would've been on that offer like a shot," added George Smith.

"I told Mr. Wilcox I needed to talk it over with Joyce first."

They all looked at him, astounded.

"You what?" Big Bill Driscoll shook his head as if trying to get water out of his ears.

"Talk it over with *Joyce*?" Andy Simmons drew back, blinking. "Joyce, your *wife*?"

"Yes, Joyce, my wife, who else?" Walter squirmed a little under their stares. "It's a big decision."

"It's a promotion!" blustered Frank. "With a considerable salary bump, might I add!"

Several of them spoke at once, an overlapping babble of "one of the youngest in the firm" and "be out of your mind not to" and "snap it right up" and "give Wilcox the wrong impression" and "opportunities like this."

"Fellas! Fellas, please!" Walter waved them down, and they subsided grudgingly. "I hear what you're saying and I know what you mean, absolutely, I do. But it *is* a big decision, one that would affect my whole family. I'd be out of town a lot for business trips and conferences, when it … heck, it already feels like I'm hardly ever at home."

"Nonsense!" declared Bill. "You're home every night, every weekend, same as the rest of us."

"Well, yes, but …" He exhaled gustily, frustrated and not sure how to get his point across. "Are we? Are we, really? We spend all day in the office, five days a week … we're out most evenings doing one thing or another"—indicating the bowling alley around them—"and on the weekends, we're so busy with our yards and cars and church … how often do we, any of us, get to just sit back and enjoy the fruits of our labors?"

"What in the Sam Hill is he on about?" Andy asked George, who shrugged.

"They say a man's home is his castle, right?" Walter pressed. "But what good's a castle if you're never even *in* it?"

"We work hard for all that," said Frank. "*Darn* hard. We bust our behinds to put roofs over our kids' heads, food on the table, give them the right kind of life—"

"I'm not arguing—"

"You're saying we should lounge around the house all day?" John challenged.

"No! No, I'm—"

"We've earned everything we've got," said Bill. "This is the gosh-darned American *Dream*!"

"To bust our behinds for houses we, what? Sleep in eight hours a night but hardly anything else?"

"To provide for our *families*!" Bill roared.

Walter stood his ground. "Families we only see at breakfast and dinner? Shouldn't they have more of *us*, more time, *real* time, real memories, instead of only what we can 'provide' for them?"

They were nose-to-nose, the rest in a circle around them. Faces were red, shoulders bunched. At any moment, someone might resort to strong language or a physical shove, which was definitely *not* how things were done here in Harmony Heights.

"Gentlemen," said Frank, very sternly. "Let's all take a step back before anybody says or does something he'll regret."

The hot glares still flashing around could have just about boiled water, but each man did ease up enough to break the tension. Belatedly, it occurred to them they had an audience: other bowlers paused in their games, the employees working the shoe counter and snack bar , the scruffy old man who swept up.

"I think I'm done for tonight," Walter said. He glanced at the rest of his team. "You fellas all right without me?"

"We'll manage," George said, his tone flat and noncommittal.

With curt nods at everyone else, Walter bagged his ball, swapped his shoes, and headed out.

———

Headed out but not home; he was in no fit state to go home just yet.

He wanted to be rational and reasonable when he talked to Joyce. It hadn't seemed right to bring up the promotion over dinner, in front of the kids. Felt ... pressuring, somehow, though whether pressuring of Joyce or pressuring of himself, he couldn't quite say.

Fact of the matter, which he certainly wasn't about to admit to anybody, was that he didn't want the promotion. Didn't want its attendant bumps in salary, title, and prestige.

Didn't, in all truth, even want the job. Hadn't wanted it in the first place. Hated it, to be totally honest. The daily aspects of the suit, the drive, the office, the paperwork, yes. But the larger aspects of it as well ... the tedium, the mundanity, the sense that none of it mattered, the unfulfilling cog-in-the-machinedness.

To just go on doing it, week after week, month after month, year after year, until he reached retirement age and took up golfing?

What kind of American Dream was that? It wasn't *his* dream. Never had been.

Yes, he had a nice house with a nice yard, but as he sat behind the wheel of his car—also nice—in the shadowed parking lot, he realized they were just pictures in his mind, without resonance, without connection. Could have been *any* house, *any* yard. And him just a stranger who happened to be there sometimes.

He had no idea what his children's rooms even looked like.

Baseball pennants and model planes for one, dolls and music boxes for the other?

He couldn't remember the last time he'd set foot in the kitchen, let alone the pantry or laundry room or Joyce's sewing room ... if Joyce even had a sewing room ... *did* she?

The foyer, front room, and dining room, he knew. The hallway and staircase. Their bedroom, with its twin beds, and master bath. He had his easy chair, his seat at the head of the table, his bed and dresser and closet.

But the rest of the house ...

A tap at the driver's side window made Walter jump and gasp in his seat. He turned his head, expecting to see Frank or George or John, come to smooth things over and persuade him to return so his team didn't have to be a man short. Which, at any other time, he may well have done, but just now, the thought of spending another single minute in the company of his so-called "friends" ...

It wasn't any of them, and he started anew at the sight of the scruffy old man who swept up. A long-term fixture at the fringes of Harmony Heights, a charity case if not quite a stew-bum, tolerated because he picked up off jobs and kept himself relatively presentable.

Roger? Gerald? Walter had seen him often enough in passing, but they'd never spoken. And to have the man tapping on his window was disconcerting, to say the least.

But maybe Frank or George had sent him. Maybe he'd stepped outside to empty the trash and noticed a flat tire Walter had somehow missed. Maybe any of a number of things. Certainly no reason to be uneasy. The old man may have been eccentric but was clearly harmless.

He rolled the window down a couple inches. "Yes?"

"I heard what you were saying in there."

A wry grin twisted the corner of Walter's mouth. Sure, him and everyone else in the bowling alley ...

"Take the promotion," the old man continued. "Don't ask your missus, don't discuss it with her. Just take it and tell her. She'll be pleased as punch."

"Excuse me? What do you know about my—?"

"What do *you*?"

"What do I what?"

"Know about her. About any of them. What they *do*. What they get up to while their hubbies are at work and their kiddies at schoo—"

"Ex*cuse* me!" Walter snapped. "I'd suggest you watch what you're—"

"And I'd suggest *you* watch! But you won't. You don't. None of you. So, take the promotion. Go on all the business trips and to all the conferences. She won't mind one bit."

"I'll thank you not to meddle in—"

"Dangit, sonny!" He pressed his callused palms flat on the window glass, maybe not as harmless as previously advertised after all. "I'm trying to help!"

"By insinuating—"

"No! No. Forget that. Just forget it. All I'm saying is it's better for everyone, the less you're at home. Leave them to their own devices. You get what you want; they get what they want."

"I don't *want* to be out of town on business trips and see my family even less than I do now!" Walter opened the door and got out, bringing himself level with the old man. "I don't *want* my son and daughter growing up hardly knowing who their father is, except as some stranger at the breakfast and dinner table!"

"Now, sir, Mr. Grady, I'm sorry—"

"I don't even want this stupid *job*!" The words burst from him, shocking Walter himself more than they did the old man, but once they were out, the dam had broken and the truth flooded forth. "I never *wanted* to sit in an office all day, pushing papers, doing meaningless *shit*!"

The vulgarity struck them both like a thunderbolt.

"All right," said the old man, cautiously, as if *Walter* were the eccentric one who might not be as harmless as previously advertised. "All right, that's fine, that's just fine—"

"No, it isn't. It isn't just fine. It isn't all right. What if I wanted to be ... to be an artist? A writer? A piano teacher? A toymaker? What if I wanted to work from home, spend time with my family? Help my wife around the house? Cook and clean and raise my children?"

"Then you're living in the wrong neighborhood, sonny. And you'd for *certain* better not breathe a single *whisper* of such notions to your missus."

"Why not? Huh?" Walter shocked himself further by taking an aggressive step, curling his fists. "Why *not*?"

Rather than flinch or look frightened, the old man sighed and hung his head, the very posture of defeat. "Well," he said. "I did try. But you don't *look*, Mr. Grady. You don't *see;* you don't *know*."

"*What*?" Walter practically snarled. "*What* don't I see or know?"

The old man raised his gaze, his eyes sad and sorrowful. "Used to live here in Harmony Heights myself, once. Had it all. The house, the wife, the kids, everything. Perfect as could be. Then ... well ... Good luck to you. Good luck to you."

With that, he turned and shuffled away, leaving Walter standing beside his car in the shadowy parking lot, utterly nonplussed.

———

There was absolutely no reason why he couldn't just go straight home.

Absolutely no reason.

Nothing preventing him.

Spend time with his family, in the house all his hard work had bought and paid for. Spend time with his children, get to know them before they grew up and the chance slipped away. Spend time with his wife, quiet time after the kids went to bed, the lights dim, the radio playing softly, sipping glasses of sherry on the couch while they talked, *really* talked. His arm around her, her head resting sweetly on his shoulder.

How long had it been since they'd done that?

Had ... had they ever done that?

Surely they must have.

They'd been young and in love, hadn't they? Full of hopes and dreams? The whole world shining fresh and new, ripe with possibilities?

There had been kisses, *real* kisses, and holding hands, hadn't there? And ... more?

Must have been!

But the memories wouldn't come, or came only in wispy fragments, more like scenes from a movie seen long ago, silver screen phantasms of another life, someone else's life.

What had happened to him, to them? To those hopes and dreams, that fresh, new world of possibilities? When had it all slipped away? Or had it ever been there to begin with? *Had* it?

If it had, could it be recaptured? Found again?

Drive straight home. Spend time with his family, his children, his wife. A man's home was his castle. Enjoy the fruits of his labors.

Absolutely nothing was stopping him. Absolutely no reason not to.

Yet ...

He couldn't.

The closer he got to Harmony Heights proper—that idyllic suburban paradise of tree-lined streets and well-kept yards and picture-perfect houses—the more his throat and chest tightened, and the more his palms sweated. A deep, pervasive sense of *wrongness* uncoiled within him and spread clammy tendrils throughout his body. His mouth felt dry, his stomach queasy.

Wrongness.

Too soon. Too early.

He wasn't supposed to be home yet. He was supposed to be out. At the bowling alley, throwing strikes and picking up spares, in fellowship and good-natured friendly competition.

Because that was the way things were done.

Walter drove on, cruising aimlessly past shopping centers and schools, gas stations and churches, the quaint old-town square with its bandstand and clock tower, other neighbor-hoods less prestigious than his own. Neighborhoods where televisions blared and babies cried and dogs barked. Where women wearing blouses and capri pants stood outside to smoke and gossip, and blue-collar workingmen sat drinking beers on their porch stoops. Where cars were obviously not washed and waxed every Saturday, some even sporting dents or patches of primer paint. Where yards were shaggy, indiffer-ently mown, afflicted with dandelions or—horror of horrors! —crabgrass.

Further on, motorcycles were canted in the gravel outside a roadhouse, the very sort of place often brought up as a subject of concern at the weekly community association meet-ings. Loud music thumped from its chocked-open doors, while leather-jacketed young men combed their slicked-back pompadours and preened in front of girls in tight sweaters. Even as he passed, a fight broke out, a scuffle of yelling and punching and thrown bottles. It reminded him of how he and Bill had nearly squared off at the bowling alley, and he flinched.

What had happened to him, to his life? Had he, or could he ever be or have been, one of those tough youths, sneering and posturing? Or a grime-knuckled laborer who carried a thermos and only wore a tie to a wedding or funeral?

Would he want to be?

The very thought made his skin crawl.

Unsettled, he began navigating his way back toward Harmony Heights, though the sense of *wrongness* in his guts told him it was still too early to be getting home.

———

"Hello, dear. How was bowling?"

The kids tucked securely into bed. The house spotless, not so much as a dirty spoon in the sink or a stray sock behind the hamper.

And there she is, still impeccable, a vision of pearls and curls, her pristine apron hung neatly on the hook behind the kitchen door, the pleats of her skirt sharp as ever, nary a rumple or wrinkle or crease to be seen.

There she is, the lovely and dutiful wife. There they are, house to house across Harmony Heights. Mary Ashton, Lois Driscoll, Betty Simmons, Joyce Grady, Peggy Parker, Ellen Smith, and so many others. The smile. The air-kiss. The patient listening, hands primly folded.

Listening to which team won, what the final scores were, the victorious strike, the abysmal gutter ball, a few light anecdotes.

No need to go into anything more. No need for unpleasantness and discord. That's not how things are done here.

"Good night, dear. You go on up; I'll be along in a minute."

His pajamas and slippers already laid out, waiting for him.

His covers already folded back, pillow plumped. He brushes his teeth, sets the alarm, gets into bed, switches off the night-stand lamp.

With the bedroom door left ajar, a mellow line of light from the hall spills across her bed.

He is sound asleep by the time her silent shadow blots out that light.

———

Except for Walter Grady.

Tired though he was, he lay wakeful, keeping his breathing slow and even, his eyelids lowered to slits.

The coffee was partly to blame. He never drank coffee so late in the day, and he didn't think he'd *ever* had coffee that packed such a wallop. Black as India ink, poured piping hot from a carafe so discolored its glass was a permanent sepia-tone, by a bubblegum-smacking waitress in a cherry-red smock.

Taking a different route to avoid passing the roadhouse again, he'd seen the diner's neon-tube glow shining scarlet through the night. Then the diner itself had come into view, a long, silvery train-car affair up on concrete blocks, its windows warm beacons, its signs offering 25-cent coffee with free refills and a "burger combo deluxe" for fifty cents.

A cup of coffee, he'd thought, would help fill the rest of the time until it was safe to go home. Only later, after he'd entered and ordered, did he stop to ponder—safe to go home? *Safe?*

Inside, the diner was checkerboard linoleum gone some-what dingy, cracked red vinyl seats, dulled chrome trim, and scuffed tabletops. Even at the odd hour, business was brisk, the counter lined with customers and most of the booths filled. A jukebox spewed rock-and-roll but at a tolerable volume. The air was thick with grease and fry-smoke.

And the coffee, as Walter quickly found out, could have kicked a hole in the Hoover Dam.

He'd gotten a corner half-booth to himself, and after a few initial glances, nobody had paid him much mind. Teens slurped milkshakes, a police officer swapped jokes with a burly man in a white paper chef's hat, third-shift workers plowed through plates of ham and eggs with hash browns, a trio of work-weary women chatted over slabs of pie.

Had he ever brought Joyce and the kids to a place like this? Somehow, he doubted it, though he couldn't be sure. *Would* he? Probably not, unless they were on vacation, driving Route 66 coast-to-coast to see this great nation of theirs, stopping at odd little roadside attractions along the way.

Had they ever done that either? Or taken in the sights at Yellowstone, Yosemite, the Grand Canyon, the Everglades?

Wasn't *that* also supposed to be part of the American Dream?

"Anything else for ya, mister?" the waitress had asked.

Not wanting to be rude or seem a skinflint, he'd ordered a piece of the apple pie and let her talk him into adding a scoop of ice cream for a mere nickel more.

He would, he'd decided, sit and drink his coffee and eat his pie, and when he was done—*when it was safe*—he'd go home.

As he sat and ate and drank, though, he began to pick up bits of the conversations going on around him, paying closer attention whenever he heard mention of Harmony Heights.

Such as ...

The police officer mentioning how it was just as well the department didn't get many calls from up there because it was, in his words, "downright creepy, too neat and tidy, everything in its place, like a dang movie set, and you hardly never see anyone out-of-doors until late afternoons."

Or the trio of women, hair frazzled, makeup faded and smudged, laughing over something one of their number had said, something about how you never saw "*those* prissy ladies" at the grocery store or gas station; heaven forbid, they might chip their nail enamel or get a run in their nylons.

Which was absurd; of *course* they went to the grocery store! Along with cooking and cleaning and ironing and mending and all the other countless tasks and errands that occupied their days.

It was jealousy; that's all it was. Jealousy, pure and simple.

*What they **do**. What they get up to while their hubbies are at work and their kiddies at school ...*

The scruffy old man's remarks recurred, and Walter angrily shook them off.

Just because he personally had never seen Joyce iron, or vacuum, or wash the windows, or scrub the bathtubs, or do the laundry ... well, obviously those things got done whether he witnessed the work or not. His shirts were always pressed, his clothes hung up and put away; everything was always spic-and-span. And just because he personally had never seen her in the actual process of cooking, only bringing complete meals to the table ...

She was efficient; that was all. Efficient in a way these women, who must have had to work second jobs as well as taking care of house and home, could only resent and view with spite and envy.

Joyce managed everything with grace and aplomb, all while maintaining her appearance and grooming. Why, he couldn't remember the last time he'd seen her without makeup, let alone with her hair in curlers. And she'd sooner be caught dead than caught in a robe or housecoat!

By the time his alarm went off every morning, she was already up and dressed and had it all under control. No matter how late he happened to stay out—if, say, poker night or the lodge meeting ran over—she waited for him, and only went to bed after he did.

He'd poked at the remnants of his pie, crumbs and amber sludge in melting ice cream. When he really sat right down and *thought* about it … combined with the mad-sounding things the old man at the parking lot had said …

*But you don't **look**, Mr. Grady. You don't see; you don't **know**.*

All I'm saying is it's better for everyone, the less you're at home. Leave them to their own devices. You get what you want; they get what they want.

*And I'd suggest **you** watch! But you won't. You don't. None of you.*

<hr>

It is how things are done here in Harmony Heights.

Serene, orderly, peaceful. All as it should be.

The pantry and refrigerator fully stocked. Always fully stocked.

All surfaces blemishless and clean. Not a speck or smudge or fingerprint to mar their perfection.

The children, well-mannered and well-behaved. Never troublesome. Should one happen to become ill or injured and need to stay home from school, there are medicines for that.

And the husbands? Dedicated, content, unquestioning.

Except …

<hr>

"Trouble sleeping, dear?"

Walter almost feigned a snore but reasoned that would only make him look foolish. He opened his eyes. "A bit."

Joyce, in the doorway, dipped her head in a genteel nod. "I'll bring you something for it."

"Joyce!" he called, throwing back the covers and sitting up.

She turned back, slowly. "Yes, dear?"

"Joyce, we need to talk."

"Aren't we talking right now?"

"Please, come and sit."

Her lips gave the merest pursed twitch, but she smoothed her skirt and sat on the twin bed opposite his. The bed where, he was more and more convinced, he'd never actually seen her sleep.

She folded her hands in her lap and looked at him. Her gaze was dark and steady, and something in it chilled Walter to the core.

"I ..." His throat clicked as he swallowed. "I was offered a promotion at work today."

Joyce's perfect eyebrows arched. "Why, that's wonderful news."

"I haven't accepted yet. I told Mr. Wilcox I needed to discuss it with you first."

The faintest of frown lines briefly furrowed her brow. "I hardly think you need my permission, dear."

"Well, it would mean a lot of business trips, conferences. Time away from you and the kids."

Did her eyes gleam just then? Or did they simply catch the light from the hallway? Had that been the beginnings of a swiftly-masked smile?

He hurried on. "I'm inclined to turn it down. In fact, I'm inclined to leave the firm altogether and find a new job which will let me work from home."

His wife went utterly motionless; he couldn't even tell if she was breathing. The nightstand clock ticked on. He reached across and clasped her hands in his. They felt cool and pliant within his grasp.

"Joyce?"

"That's not how things are done here, Walter."

"Why not? It ... it could be." He tried a feeble smile. "I'd be here, with you and the kids. To help out with chores and errands. To let us spend more time together, as a family."

"Chores and errands," she repeated tonelessly.

"The shopping, cleaning, cooking—"

"There are no chores and errands."

"Excuse me?"

She tightened her grip, which was surprisingly strong, almost painful. "Leave it be," she told him. "Accept the promotion and let us go on as we have been. You mustn't rock the boat."

"Boat? What boat? Joyce, what do you mean?"

"Do you remember our wedding?"

The question threw him even further off balance, a state not helped by realizing, no matter how he wracked his brains ... that ... that he ... no, he didn't.

"Do you remember the children being born?" Joyce continued. "Do you remember them as babies, toddlers?"

"I ..."

"Yet, here we are," she said. "A home. A family. Your meals, your clothes, your drink after work, everything taken care of. An ideal life. Isn't that what you want?"

You get what you want; they get what they want, the old man whispered in his memory.

"And what do *you* want?" Walter asked. He fitfully shook his head. "Who ... *what* even *are* you, Joyce?"

"I'm telling you for the last time, *dear*—" Her enameled nails dug in. "Leave it be. Forget all this. You will, easily enough, if you let yourself."

He ignored that, and the crescents of pain indenting his skin. "What do you *do* while I'm gone all day? If there are no

89

chores and errands, if it's all just ... How did you put it? Taken care of? Taken care of how? By whom?"

She softened both grip and gaze. "Walter. Please."

"What *is* all this? Who *are* you?" He tightened *his* grip then, suddenly not caring if he frightened or hurt her. "*What* are you? *Tell* me, Joyce! Tell me, damn you!"

"Since you insist," she said, "I'll *show* you."

———

"Kids! Breakfast!"

Waffles and sausage links and scrambled eggs, orange juice and milk.

Innocent questions.

"Why, your father's away on a business trip. He got an important promotion at work. And while it may mean we don't see him as much, we should all be very, very proud."

Eager questions.

"Quite a bit more, yes. A what? Oh, sweetheart. Perhaps not a puppy, but how about a new bike?"

Worried questions.

"Of course he does. Of course he will. And, if not, well, we'll just get another."

Puzzled questions.

"Absolutely. That's how things are done. But, my goodness, look at the time! Mustn't be late!"

Lunches and book bags, and out the door they go, skipping along the sidewalk to join the happy tide of children rushing to meet the sunshine-yellow school bus.

Clear blue skies, green lawns, white picket fences, rose-pink flowers.

Not long after, from other houses, the husbands. Hats and briefcases. Cars backing down driveways. Wives poised on porches, waving, beatific. Pristine aprons, pleated dresses, heels and pearls, makeup flawless, not a curl out of place.

The neighborhood empties. A hush falls but for the rustle of leaves in the breeze and the amiable twitter of birds.

Across well-kept yards and clean, quiet streets, the wives exchange glances. They share secret smiles.

Then, as one, they turn and step back inside. The doors close.

It's looking to be another perfect day, here in Harmony Heights.

Family Traits

By Chantell Renee

Sun kissed the rosy cheeks of the playing children. Kites sored in the air as the youthful voices sang, "Red Rover, Red Rover, send Ellie right over!" Screams of laughter erupted as the small girl tried and failed to break the hand-in-hand human chain of the opposite team apart. Little Ellie quickly ran down the line to join the new team, swinging her arm as she grabbed the hand of the boy at the end.

Jane watched her children playing with the others. With a smile on her face, she pushed down the urge to stand up and leave the large gathering. Someplace, her husband, Frank, chewed the fat with the other men of the church. How had she made it this far? Tabbitha, her seven-year-old, was called over in the game next. She didn't break the chain either and was absorbed by the opposite team too.

"Well, aren't they having a ball," a female voice she recognized as Nickey Grinner's said.

"Hey, Nickey. I suppose they are." The bottom of Jane's

lip found its way between her teeth, a habit she'd worked hard to rid herself of but hadn't succeeded.

"I see your husband made it in time for tomorrow's celebrations. Another big birthday for our great nation." Jane looked over at Nickey, who was helping herself to an eyeful of Frank.

See, she thought, *even this one would have loved to marry him.*

He was truly handsome. Close to six-two, built like a dancer, Frank Mareno had been her husband for just over a decade. Her own eyes moved over him, and bile lifted in her throat as his eyes met hers. She looked away.

"You are a lucky girl, Jane," Nickey said, a little breathless. She pulled out a cigarette and held the pack up for Jane to help herself.

"Oh, no, thank you. I've quit." Her lip sucked in between her teeth, and she bit down. Her eyes shot toward her husband, but if he'd been watching, she'd not know until later.

━━

His bags were already packed though, he'd only gotten in that morning. When had he done that? He'd taken the kids to his mother's all day. Frank was a much better father now that the kids had grown out of diapers. Though it hadn't stopped his mother from correcting Jane's mothering. Not that she tried much anymore. The kids didn't respect her or call her mother. Why would they? The Mareno family never considered Jane anything more than the vessel they used to produce the grandbabies, according to the last thing her husband had said that morning when she asked if she needed to go with them that day. Of course, he'd wanted her to stay home and get the meat ready for the big celebration in a couple days. But it was still frozen, and it was too early.

She'd been fifteen when she got pregnant, though Frank told everyone she'd been seventeen. Besty Mareno didn't care. Jane's bloodline was tied to the late Thomas Gaetano, the visionary who gathered the families in the big city and divided it all up into territories which were making a lot of people rich. Even though her mother had chosen to leave that life, having the blood of one of the Big Five Families made Jane important for the Mareno family plans. Only a few people knew this, but it was the right people who did know. The perfect way to have their cake and eat it too.

What would happen when the kids were old enough and didn't need a caregiver? Would they keep her around or ...?

Looking down at his bags, her foot shot out and kicked at the thick brown leather case. The top came apart—he'd not buttoned it correctly. Green paper money caught her eye. Squatting close, she pulled the thick lips of the case apart. More money than she'd ever seen before lay in piles inside the case. A white envelope peeked out between the leather case and the bills. She tugged it out and pulled a single piece of crisp white folded paper, a note, from the envelope. Frank's handwriting indicated the purpose of the letter. "Dear Jane ..."

"Frank, I hear you plan on bringing some big cuts of meat for tomorrow?" Bill smiled at the taller man. He lipped his can of beer, then took a swig.

"You bet." Frank hated Bill. He was a weasel. Always nosing around, trying to keep tabs on his comings and goings. Then he remembered Texas was only a couple days drive away, and the fresh irritation left him. Bill could poke his nose where the fuck ever he wanted. Soon it wouldn't affect him in any way. He'd done his familial duty; time for him to have the life he wanted.

"So, Frank, when ya heading back on the road?" one of the other guys from their group asked. He didn't remember the man's name. They may have played some poker together at some point.

"I'm thinking tomorrow after the food. Roads will be cleared with everyone shooting off the fireworks." Frank smiled.

"How's the life of a traveling salesman treating you and yours?" Rob asked. Or was it Bob?

"Great. Really great." Frank thought of pale, taut skin, eyes the color of the sky. Texas was so close.

"Hey, we're gonna pull the dogs and burgers off the grill for the kiddies. If ya have anything to toss on the grill a little early ..." Bill called as he stacked sizzling patties on top of one another. Frank wagged a finger at the man.

Just then he looked up and met the dull brown eyes of his wife. She had aged so much in the last ten years. He had noticed lines around her mouth from all the smoking she'd been doing the last year. His fist clenched at the thought of her sagging breasts, flat ass. Why couldn't he have just made the babies with her and left? His mother insisted they be married. If he thought about it, the bigger family wouldn't consider his son a rightful heir if he was out of wedlock. That cooled his anger. Besides, all the years he'd given to this hairbrained idea meant he had that much more time to be with his Texas Rose. The kids would be fine with his family, and he'd be back for them at some point to move closer to New York.

"Oh no, no sneak peeks. Don't worry, it'll be worth the wait." He did his best salesman smile, then walked away, tossing his full can of beer in the trash can.

The kids came in and changed. Their grandmother was there to take them shopping after the Sunday festivities. Jane heard the front door shut. Frank came into the room. She was surprised Frank didn't go. But she was fine with it; she had some things to ask him.

"They have really grown. I told Mom to keep them for the night." He walked past her as she flipped the light in the bathroom off. That room was done, one less thing to do before she got started.

"You've missed a lot." Her mind spun with the words that had been on that sheet of paper. She wasn't sure how she'd waited a full day to mention it, but she had.

"What the fuck is that supposed to mean, Jane?" His tone snapped her out of her own anger.

"Nothing, I was just agreeing with you." She needed to be smarter. What should she say to him?'

"You have a mouth on you, don't you?" He laughed, but she didn't see the usual malice in his glare. He was different. And she knew exactly why. Tightness gripped her skin, causing her to flush red.

"Is she pregnant?" The words came out without warning.

"What?" He truly looked flabbergasted.

"Texas?" Since that's how he'd referred to her in the letter.

"Aww, so you went snooping?" There, the gleam of hate she'd grown used to seeing in his eyes the last year appeared.

"Unintentionally. But I know now. What about your kids?" She felt the strength in speaking her truth.

"There, see! Your kids? They are OUR kids." He spat at her. Before she could retort, his fist slammed into her ribs. Air left her lungs, and she fell back, hitting the hardwood floor. Her head spun as she gasped for oxygen. Choking, she tried to roll onto her side.

He pushed her back to the floor, pinning her down with his foot; it hurt, but the sudden move forced her shoulders apart, allowing her lungs to fill once more. "Listen to me, cunt. You will raise OUR kids. My mother will be here watching you. She will take them from you and toss you out on your ass if you step one hair out of line. When and if I decide, I'll come back some day. And if my Rose is with child, she will be the mother you failed to be for them." He slapped her face. Not hard enough to leave a bruise but hard enough to cause her cheek to swell. He was an expert at making it hurt but not show.

"I won't do it," she said, but her voice was low. Frank had already moved to the door and didn't hear her retort.

"Get some ice; the picnic is tomorrow. And stay away from that Nickey bitch and her cigarettes," he called as he walked down the hallway.

"I won't do it," she whispered to herself.

"Are you serious? This is way more than we thought we'd be getting!" Bob waved over to some of the other men to help him get the containers of marinated meat out of the back of the Ford Squire.

"You know the Marenos, only the best," Jane said, touching her sore rib cage. She saw Bob notice, but he quickly looked away. They all did that. Don't see, don't tell. The moto of their congregation.

"We have other meat, though ..." Bob ran a hand over his chin.

Jane felt a little flip in her stomach; there couldn't be any left after today.

"Come now, Bob. You know we'll be having that big Mass after Pioneer Day. Let's just freeze it in that big ole freezer the church just got. It's only a few weeks away. Unless you think the

Marenos won't mind tossing some of this to the wild ..." She *lowered her voice, making it seem less savory of an idea.*

"You know what? We have plenty of room in the freezer for the other meat. Plus, this is seasoned and ready to go. Okay, guys, let's get this inside." Bob hadn't missed a beat, and she was pleased. Phase one was finished. He didn't look her in the eyes once. If he had, he would have seen the slight swelling in her cheek. But the avoidance wasn't surprising by now.

"Jane, Grandma said for you and Dad to sit with her today."

She looked at her only son. She hated Frank more for making her despise her own child. Jimmy hadn't wanted anything to do with her since he had turned six. Of course, Grandma had taken them as much as she could and spoiled them horribly. Now, the boy had the idea he was a little prince. She never understood why her father hadn't gone to her mother's family to help her when he'd gotten sick. Now, she did. People like the Marenos only cared about things that made their own lives easier. If there was something in it for them, then and only then would something be done.

"Tell your grandmother your father left already and that I have to get home and get the sowing ready. I'll come back by for the fireworks."

The boy looked put out but walked away with zero empathy for his mother. If he only knew "sowing ready" had become code for "I have bruises and can't be seen in public."

———

The cold water soaked into the washcloth. Cold water numbed her fingers as she wrung out the cloth and pressed it to her cheek. From down the hallway, she heard the television set turn on. The half of lamb carcass he'd brought her to prepare was waiting for her on a slab of ice. The metal table with the thick piece of marble that the lamb lay on was an embalming table. When he'd gotten the undertakers table for her to use for butchering, she'd thought he was insane. However, with the pulley system he'd installed over the sink and the wheels on the legs, it made the work much easier than her father had had it all those years ago. Both the table and deep freezer had been pricy but had saved them a lot of money over the years. If her father hadn't taught her the craft so well, she probably wouldn't have made it this long with Frank. One had to be useful to a man in some way, especially a man like him.

Slowly, she made her way to the kitchen, making sure to avoid Frank, and put on her butcher apron. Quietly, she opened the cupboards and retrieved her oil can. The wheels of the embalming table didn't squeak much, but even the smallest sound would bring Frank into the room looking to take his frustrations out on her. After the wheels were done, she softly closed the door, knowing the sounds of the work would be muffled enough.

The farmer had skinned and bled the animal already, so there was only the cutting left. She got to work, picking the chopping knife up first from the long row of sharp implements. As she worked, her mind went back to her father.

"Now pay attention, Jane." Her father's thick hands hung the incapacitated lamb upside down. At night, he'd complained about his back, and now she could see why. The thing was small but was probably a good fifty pounds.

"Daddy, what's the lamb's name?"

"Jane, you know this is not a pet. He is food. He is how we make money to put food on our own table." His tone wasn't patronizing but matter-of-fact. She understood. Her kitten was a pet; this was food. He carefully lifted a sharp blade and slid it across the neck of the white fluffy creature. Blood, red and thicker than she'd expected it to be, splashed to the floor and began to pour down the drain. Soon, there was no more blood save for a few drips.

"Okay, Jane, we have exsanguinated the animal. That means we have ended his life to help us live by draining him of his blood. This is the way my grandfather's father fed his people when there was nothing but trees and dirt on this very land." His dark skin crinkled as he smiled at her. She loved it when he spoke about their people. Though he didn't do it often and had made her promise to never talk about it outside of their home or in front of others. Because her mother had been so fair, Jane didn't look native.

"On the neck," she recited.

"Only on the left side, where the heart is, baby girl." He used the knife to mimic what he had done. "Now, what do we say to this creature?"

"Thank you for your life. We will honor you by using every part of you." And they would. Her father had buyers for every part of the thing, even the eyeballs. Now that she was eight, she was in charge of wrapping up the parts.

"Perfect." Her father smiled at her. He was the last man in her life to show her kindness.

"Are you fucking joking? Where is all the meat?" Frank had come into the kitchen quietly. Jane turned around; he glared at her. Instinctively, she stood still.

"This is all of the meat." Confusion spread over her brow.

"I brought you a healthy fucking lamb, and this is all you have?" He walked over to the counter and knocked the freshly cut meat to the ground. She smelled it then, the whisky. He lunged toward her, and she jerked back out of his reach. The buttons of her polyester blouse busted, and her ample breast appeared. Instantly, she grabbed her blouse and tried to pull it together and leave the room.

He was faster than she was; his hairy arms encircled her and threw her to the side. She landed on the freshly cleaned embalming table. Being slight of build, she felt the connection with the large piece of marble throughout her body. However, there was no time for recovery. Frank was there, lifting her fully onto the table and climbing on top of her.

"No!" Her blood turned cold, but her senses alerted her; this wasn't just him taking what he wanted. After all, he didn't want her; he wanted Texas.

Strong hands pushed her down, ripping off her blouse and pushing her skirt up. As he drove inside of her, ignoring her weak attempts to get him off of her, his left hand grasped her throat. This was the signal—stop or I'll hurt you worse. So, she did. Except his fingers got tighter instead of moving away. Both his hands grasped her neck now; his thrusts grew harder.

Jane felt her body needing the air being denied to it, the abuse of the sex. Her hands moved around, and there, next to her right hand, the small handle of a knife. Without any thought, she plunged it into the spot her father had shown her all those years ago. Franks eyes grew wide, his sight focused, unlike he'd been when he'd started the attack. His hands flew to his own neck, then he fell. Coughing, Jane dropped off the table and scurried to the corner of the kitchen. A few minutes passed; she worked at getting her breathing under control.

When she stood up, the scene nearly made her fall back to the floor. Frank lay still on his side, blood pooled around him. Most of the lamb lay on the floor, blood slowly engulfing the neatly cut meat. A squeaking noise caught her attention. Her hazel eyes lifted up to the pully. For some reason, it swung. However, the pain in her body coupled with the irrational terror of her mother-in-law showing up unannounced made her ignore the reason the device moved. There was only one thing she could do, and the thought caused her more joy than she'd had in years.

The last of Frank's blood slid down the sink.

"Thank you, Frank, for providing for your family and

town. I will honor you by using every part of you." She lowered him onto the embalming table. "Yes, thank you so very much, Frank."

⸺

"These ribs are amazing!" Nickey boasted as she tore another mouthful off the bones.

Jane watched as the congregation devoured her family's contributions.

"Nickey, I haven't thanked you enough for all that you've done for me. I truly don't know how I could have done it without you." Jane knew the woman would see the faint bruising on her cheek. She knew she'd seen all the things all those years, just like everyone that surrounded them had. If she thought about it, she was sure Nickey had intentionally influenced her to do many things that might cause her husband to not want her anymore. But the other woman would never have gotten a man like Frank. She was too tartish for him. And maybe she knew that too.

Nickey smiled and cocked her head with faux appreciative acknowledgment. She had taken another large bite of the rib. Someplace, children laughed.

"Enjoy, I need to get on home."

Nickey simply wiped at her mouth and smiled. Jane paused, hoping she might actually say something to comfort her. But the woman turned to Diane and struck up a conversation. Just like she expected she would.

Quietly, Jane made her way down the lawn in the darkness. Fireworks flew into the sky; cheers accompanied the popping.

The highway snaked northeast. All those years, Jane wondered how Frank could stand all that driving. Now, she understood. With each mile she left behind her, she felt herself coming to life. Freedom. No plans, no real direction, but she was free. As the easy motion of the drive settled her nerves, she wondered how long it might take for them to notice she wasn't there. And once they did, how long would it take for them to find the treasure she'd left in the freezer?

Part of her felt wrong for leaving it, but technically, she did use it for a purpose. After all, how would his loving family ever realized what had become of their son if she'd not left something of him for them to find? The thought of his frozen eyes looking up at his mother brought her great joy. The thrill of the smaller part of him she'd left in his mouth would be between her and the men of the town. That was true art. Perhaps there was a little of her mother's family traits in her after all.

Blueberry Buckle

Caitlin Marceau

The knife cuts through the cake, the soft pastry dotted with stains of indigo parting for the sharp stainless steel, bits of cinnamon crumble rolling off onto the counter. She slides the knife under the slice and lifts it onto a small side plate before carrying it and a dessert fork out to her husband in the dining room.

Russell grumbles something as she sets the cake down on the placemat in front of him. She's tempted to ask him to repeat what he said but decides that he can keep whatever backhanded remark he's made. He's always unpleasant to be around when he comes home late from work, his body sore from the hard labour of manufacturing freight carts and his mood soured from a long day spent being ordered around by his shift manager.

He picks the fork up with clumsy fingers, the metal slipping out of his grip and banging loudly against the cream melamine plate. He huffs in annoyance and grabs the slice of cake with his bare hand, cramming it into his mouth and taking a bite. He chews, his tobacco-yellow teeth grinding the pastry down into wet mush, before swallowing it with a grimace.

"This is shit," he tells her as she takes a seat across from him at the table.

Birdie goes to take a sip of her wine but realizes with sadness that the glass is empty. Normally, she'd get up to get some more, but she's too tired to be bothered. Instead, she leans back in her seat and places a hand on her stomach, enjoying the way her skin moves as the baby kicks and pushes against her.

Russell waits for her to answer, but she knows better than that.

"This is *shit*," he says again, louder this time.

She looks up at him, her eyes locked with his, but keeps her mouth shut.

"This isn't my grandmother's recipe."

It's not a question.

He slams his hands on the table and spits the masticated cake out onto the plate, pushing it away from him roughly.

"I said I wanted blueberry buckle."

"And you *got* blueberry buckle," she tells him, unfazed.

"You know what I meant!" he booms.

The floor squeaks from behind her, and at the sound of it, Birdie holds on to the table for support and pushes herself up out of her seat. She turns, frowning at the small child that stands in the doorway of the dining room.

"Judy, it's bedtime. You know you're not supposed to be up this late."

"I just wanted some water."

Russell laughs unkindly.

"So you can piss the bed again?" he laughs.

"No. I—"

"Come on." Birdie crosses the room to her daughter and guides her back down the hall towards the kitchen.

She takes a glass out of the cupboard and fills it a quarter of the way with water before handing it to Judy. She eagerly gulps it down, the glass looking much too big in the small girl's hands.

"How many times do I have to tell you to stay in your room when your dad comes home late?" she asks, brushing a strand of curly red hair out of Judy's face and tucking it behind her ear.

"But I was thirsty."

"I know, sweetie."

"Can I have more?"

Birdie shakes her head. "I don't want you to wake up in the middle of the night needing to use the bathroom."

Judy's full pink lips curl into a small frown.

"Okay," she says, her disappointment making the word long and drawn out.

Birdie gives a small smile and bends down, a hand resting on her back for support as she kisses the top of her head.

"I love you, sweetie. Have a good sleep," she says, standing back up and taking the empty cup from her daughter.

Judy flings her arms out and tries to get them around her mother's waist, the side of her face resting against her bulging tummy, before letting go and scampering off to bed. As much as Birdie has grown to hate Russell over the last four years, she's grateful that he gave her a beautiful daughter and soon—God willing—a son.

Not wanting to deal with the drunkard waiting for her in the other room, she turns her attention to cleaning up the rest of the cake. She puts the blueberry buckle into a Tupperware container, trying not to smoosh it down too badly with the lid, before putting it on the counter next to the fridge. She lightly dampens the sponge by the sink and runs it over the smooth blue laminate when her husband's heavy footsteps make their way toward her.

Russell holds the plate with one hand and throws it at the sink, the plastic slamming hard against the metal, bits of cake showering the freshly cleaned space.

"I *told you* I wanted blueberry buckle, and you *knew* that I wanted you to make it with the family recipe."

"You never said that—"

"You *knew* what I wanted," he says with a low voice, taking a step towards Birdie.

She knows he's trying to intimidate her, trying to frighten her, and normally it wouldn't work. But now ...

She places her hand protectively on her stomach and holds her ground, locking eyes with his. Time feels like it's standing still between them, but the illusion is broken once he speaks.

"You're going to make the right fucking dessert tomorrow. And Judy's going to help you."

Birdie's throat tightens and her knees go weak.

"She's only four."

"I've seen her help you in the kitchen."

"With stirring and measuring, not—"

"She's old enough," he says firmly.

Birdie opens her mouth, but nothing comes out.

———

Judy shifts her weight from one foot to the next as she stands beside her mom at the kitchen counter. She does as Birdie instructs, measuring the flour slowly and combining it with the baking powder and salt. She stirs it with a fork, kicking up small clouds of white and slowing down when her mother tells her to be careful. In another ceramic bowl, she scoops in the sugar as directed. Birdie then helps her crack and deshell an egg, dropping it in.

"Do you remember your Great-Grandma MacLean, sweetie?" Birdie asks softly.

Judy shrugs, her eyes focused on the length of black leather wound tightly on the counter nearby.

"She died when you were very little. Littler than you are now," she says, her words sticking to the back of her throat as she forces them out. "You met her a few times. She was very small and had long grey hair that fell almost all the way down her back."

Birdie doesn't mention that Great-Grandma MacLean wasn't short so much as she was bent over, her back twisted and gnarled like the trunk of a tree. She doesn't explain that the woman's hair was so thin and spindly that the strands of grey used to remind her of spider legs kicking and wiggling on their own accord.

"Oh."

It's all that Judy can muster for the woman she never really knew.

"Years ago, when Great-Grandma MacLean was just a young woman, she endured a terrible hardship," Birdie says.

She recites the story from memory.

She recites it the way all MacLean women, be they MacLeans by blood or by marriage, are taught to.

"Her husband was sick, they were poor, and she had a son to feed. It was a harsh winter and food was scarce, but they made do. Then spring came, and just when things looked like they were going to get better, her husband died and left her a widow."

Birdie walks across the room to the fridge and takes out two small containers of blueberries, picked fresh from her yard, while Judy follows close at her heels. She sets them down next to the sink, where a colander is already waiting inside the deep metal basin, and motions for the young girl to come closer. Birdie turns the tap on and holds her hand under the stream, making sure the water is cool but not cold.

"Unable to afford a funeral, Great-Grandma MacLean did the only thing she could do. She dragged the body of her husband to the edge of her land and buried him deep in the ground."

Once the water is ready, she turns the first container of berries into the colander and gently begins to wash them, showing her daughter how to move them carefully with her hand without crushing the delicate fruit between her fingers or against the metal dish. Satisfied that Judy knows what to do, she leaves the girl to continue washing while she lines a heavy ceramic bowl with a clean kitchen towel to dry the berries in. After a moment, she empties the colander into the bowl and has Judy wash the second batch of berries all on her own.

"Great-Grandma MacLean was sure she and her son were doomed. Although the harsh cold had finally let up and a warm summer meant they could live off the land, they were destitute and she had no plan for when winter came again. But then a miracle happened! Scores of blueberries began to grow where Great-Grandpa MacLean had been buried, and she knew they were saved."

Judy carries the bowl of fruit over to the counter and sets it down next to the other ones.

"Instead of selling the blueberries, which she knew would run out quickly, she baked them into goods. She had some flour and sugar left from winter, eggs from her scrawny chicken, and the berries from the earth."

Judy watches anxiously as Birdie walks to the other side of the room and opens one of the drawers, the kitchen tools clinking and clanking against themselves as they slide around inside. She takes out a butcher's knife, the curved, sharp blade ending ominously in a point, and sets it on the counter in front of her child.

"But she was too poor to even afford lard, and she had no pigs to cull."

Birdie wipes her hands on the front of her half-apron before picking up the leather from the counter, the long belt unravelling as she holds it up for Judy to see. She gives her daughter a small smile before slowly kneeling on the floor. It's a difficult process, her centre of gravity thrown off, thanks to the weight of the baby, but once she makes it onto the ground, she pushes Judy's dress above her knees.

"Just when Great-Grandma MacLean was about to give up hope, she remembered that her husband's death, his *sacrifice*, gave her the bountiful harvest of blueberries. And now, it was her turn to make a sacrifice."

Birdie ties the belt around Judy's left thigh, tightening it until it's slightly uncomfortable—but not painful—around her pink skin. She then begins to pantomime cutting into Judy's leg while the girl watches nervously, her little hands balled up against her chest.

"She cut a strip out of her thigh. From that flesh, she separated the fat from the sinew and rendered it over a fire for hours. When she was done, she used the fat to make her first blueberry buckle. She gave away samples to her neighbours and brought slices into town for the store owners to try. It was so delicious that she limped home with almost thirty orders."

She waits for Judy to say something, but the girl's eyes are fixed anxiously on the knife.

She's seen Birdie's scars.

"Great-Grandma MacLean's sacrifice saved her family. And so we MacLean women honour her memory by giving up a piece of ourselves whenever we make this recipe. *All* the MacLean women learn how to make hard sacrifices. Do you understand?"

Judy nods her head and braces for the knife.

The blade cuts through the cake, the soft pastry splitting apart and dotting the counter with crumbs. Birdie lifts the massive slice onto the melamine plate before balancing a fork on the edge next to it. She picks the dish up and carries it back to the dining room, placing it in front of Russell at the table before taking a seat across from him.

He leans forward and squints, examining the food. His face is so close to the pastry that his nose is practically enveloped by cake.

"It's her recipe?"

"Yes."

He looks up at her and raises an eyebrow.

"If you're lying, I'll know."

"I said it was hers."

Russell puts the plate back on the table and stabs it with the fork.

"And Judy helped? Judy *contributed*?"

"Yes," Birdie says, fists clenched in her lap.

Russell smiles to himself, as if amused at the thought of his daughter in pain for his meal.

"Good."

He lifts the skewered cake to his mouth and stuffs it in past his lips. He chews the cake for longer than he needs to, like a cow working its cud, and eventually swallows. He gives her a wide grin that doesn't reach his eyes.

"Delicious."

Russell eats the cake in silence that's punctuated only by the sound of his wet smacking lips. Once he's done with his slice, he pounds on the table with his fist, letting her know he wants another one. It takes Birdie a minute to get up from her seat, the weight of the baby inside of her feeling especially heavy tonight as she goes to fetch him more cake. This time, she scoops an even larger slice onto his plate, knowing he'll be greedy for it.

Like the last piece, she sets it down in front of him and returns to her spot at the table to watch.

As expected, Russell eats it down, barely making time to breathe between bites, and slams his fist on the table for more.

Birdie slowly gets up and grabs his plate, heading back into the kitchen. She heaps another massive slice of the blueberry buckle onto the dish and carries it back to him. As she sets it down on the table, she notices that his forehead and neck are coated in sweat.

She smiles as she takes a seat across from him once more.

Russell takes a bite and slowly chews the cake but stops abruptly as he begins to cough, showering the table in specks of wet pastry. Once he finishes coughing, he gulps down air through his open mouth. Revulsion twists inside of Birdie, her eyes finding the bits of royal blue stuck between his teeth from half-eaten berries.

"Don't you like it?" she asks, pointing to what's left on his plate.

He doesn't answer. Instead, he closes his eyes and grips the table with a hand, trying to steady himself as his breathing grows more laboured. He puts a hand on his chest and grabs at his shirt.

"Call ... the ... oper ... ator." His words come out slow and measured as he speaks, trying not to choke.

His face is pale and splotchy as sweat runs down his skin. It soaks into the collar of his dirty work shirt, and the excessive perspiration darkens the fabric of his underarms. His eyes are wide with concern but dark with anger.

"I ... said ... call ... the ..."

Birdie waits for him to keep talking, but when the pause

grows and stretches into maintained silence, she realizes he can't. The muscles around his jaw are clenched tight, making speech impossible. He grips the table harder and moans as his back and neck begin to spasm and cramp. He stares at her, waiting for help, but when she remains seated across from him, he realizes he's on his own.

Russell tries to get up from the table, but his muscles are so badly constricted that he falls to his knees the second he lifts himself from the chair. He reaches out for the table, hoping to grab on to the edge of it to hoist himself up, but his body begins to shake and convulse painfully. His grease-stained hand curls around the cloth placemat, and he drags it, and the blueberry buckle, onto the floor with him. He stares at the ceiling, eyes wide in pain, as his body quivers. The air whistles as it moves in and out of his nostrils, his breathing fast.

Birdie slowly gets out of her seat and makes her way over to him, rubbing her thigh and grimacing from the pain as she moves. She nudges his stomach with the tip of her house shoe and quickly takes a step back, worried he might still be able to grab her. He tries to reach out, but his stiff and cramped muscles make it so that he only manages a weak flail.

She feels Russell's eyes on her as she looms over him, his gaze making its way up her legs. Even prostrated on the floor, he can't help but peek under the hem of her shirtwaist dress, catching a flash of white. His eyes widen with realization, and she smiles down at him, lifting the cotton hem high enough for him to get a good look at the bandage wrapped around her skin and the tufts of white gauze stained with red.

"Did you really think I'd mutilate *my* daughter like that? Did you really think I'd hurt *my* baby for *you*?"

He tries to speak, but the words get compressed and flattened into noise as he convulses again.

"You'd think after hearing your grandma's story so often —after seeing your own mother cut herself open again and again—you'd understand the moral of it all," she spits. "It's never been about keeping the men of the family full and satisfied. It's never even been about honouring her memory. It's been about honouring the sacrifice a *mother* made to keep her *child* safe."

Words form at the back of Russell's throat but come out through his teeth in a hiss.

The floor squeaks behind them as Judy makes her way into the room. She hides behind her mother, holding on to the fabric of her skirts as she peers around Birdie to look down at her father.

"It's okay, sweetie; you don't have to be nervous. We talked about this, remember?"

Judy nods her head.

"Go on, tell your father what you learned today."

"That we *all* need to make sacrifices," she says quietly against her mother's hip.

"That's my girl. Now help me get his hands."

———

It takes Birdie a long while to drag Russell through the house.

Between the weight of his limp body and the weight of her pregnant one, it's a slow process to roll him onto the bed sheet and drag him across the hardwood. He tries to put up a fight more than once, but the convulsions and cramping make it impossible for him to do more than flop and writhe like a caught fish.

To Birdie's relief, whatever fight he had left leaves his body as they pull him through the door to the backyard. She looks around, trying to understand what's knocked the wind from his sails, when she sees the empty bottle on the grass with the bright yellow label: Dave's Miracle Strychnine Gopher Corn.

Once outside, she and Judy wrestle the bulk of Russell

onto an old wooden toboggan they found in the garage and make short work of dragging him to the edge of the property.

Waiting for him by the blueberry bushes is a deep pit.

"Didn't Great-Grandma MacLean bury Great-Grandpa MacLean in the spring?" Judy asks, helping to push the sled to the edge of the hole.

"She did."

"So shouldn't *we* wait until spring?"

Birdie slowly gets down onto the grass and pushes Russell into the grave. She's not even aware that he's still alive until he hits the bottom and lets out a moan of pain, his body twitching and shaking as another seizure passes through him.

"No, sweetie," Birdie says gently, her thigh aching where her flesh used to be.

"But what about the blueberries? Will they still grow big and sweet if we do this now?"

She looks at Judy and smiles, admiring the way her curls bounce in the summer breeze and how her big eyes sparkle in the moonlight. She takes her daughter's soft hands in her own and smiles.

"I think they'll grow to be the sweetest berries yet."

Bait

By Miracle Austin

October 13, 1959 ... the last time I would ever see Jimmy Lee, my husband.

Attempting to keep myself alive for our unborn baby, I held my breath for over one hundred and eighty seconds. Before my arms and legs ceased their final movements, as I sank down deeper and deeper into the ice-cold water, my eyes started closing. I felt something brush up against my legs. Within seconds, everything became blurry, and my mind drifted back to past memories I wanted to erase before I took my last breath.

I wish I'd never laid eyes on Jimmy Lee at the Cypress Hills High School winter sock hop. I was only fifteen when I first saw him strolling into the gym carrying boxes on his muscular shoulders. His fitted, cuffed black jeans and T-shirt highlighted his chiseled body. His pompadour was perfect, not one hair out of place. Jimmy Lee's light brown eyes with thick eyebrows and curly lashes locked on mine as he passed by me and my best friend, Geraldine, sitting on the bottom bleacher.

Chewing bubble gum and humming, "Please Send Me Someone To Love" by Percy Mayfield, I asked, "Who's that?"

Geraldine leaned in closer to whisper in my ear. "Oh, that's Jimmy Lee. He graduated from St. John's Academy last year. He was captain of the basketball team and glee club. He's so dreamy. I heard he just broke up with his steady and he's available."

"Thank you for the scoop, Geraldine." I stood up, twirling around in my pink and blue poodle skirt, popping my gum, and called out, "Hey, good lookin' ... what you got cookin' ..." I plopped back down.

He stopped, turned around, and approached us.

"Now, let me see. Which doll out the two of ya said that?" he asked, stroking his chin. He grinned, and his deep dimples appeared out of nowhere.

I gulped, my eyes growing wide. I blew out a huge bubble. He poked it, then wrapped *my* gum around his finger and inserted it into his mouth. I gasped.

He looked over at Geraldine and asked, "What's her name?"

"That's Valerie. My best friend. I call her Val for short—only her good friends call her that. I gave her that nickname when I first met her in second grade," Geraldine rambled.

"Hello, Val," he said, crouching down to my eye level, and then looked over at Geraldine. "Hey, Geraldine, you look like a doll who likes chocolate shakes with the works?"

"I sure do, Jimmy Lee," she said, blinking her eyes.

"Follow me to the cafeteria, then. I got a friend who makes the best shakes in town," he said. "Hey, Val, I'm going to deliver these boxes to the back. Stay right here and don't move. Save the rest of the dances for me."

I should've known the first time I met Jimmy Lee that he

would be trouble for me, but I never imagined he would be the *near* death of me. He proposed a year later, and we were married before my senior year in high school. I didn't graduate because he landed a job at his uncle's business as a salesman in Rhode Island.

He was so loving and caring during our first two years of marriage. Everything changed when I became pregnant with our first child; he began leaving me home alone when he wasn't working. Our first baby was stillborn. Jimmy Lee told me how we really didn't need children anyhow because they would only stifle our marriage and get in the way. A year later, I was pregnant again.

My grandmom warned me about Jimmy Lee. She told me on her deathbed how the Lees had always been trouble. Now, I wish I'd listened to her. Before she departed, she told me about a cousin I had in Puerto Rico and to call him if I ever needed anything. He would know exactly what to do. She gave me his number and instructed me to memorize it.

Jimmy Lee always told me I was cruisin' for a bruisin' before he left his personal signatures on my upper arms, torso, inner thighs, or face. I hid my bruises by wearing long sleeves, head scarfs, sunglasses, and concealing my face with makeup as best as I could. If my black eyes or swollen lips were too pronounced to go out in public, then I would pretend to be ill until the swelling went down.

Keeping our house spotless, ironing his clothes with perfection, satisfying only his expectations, and exquisite dinners for his friends or business partners, sometimes at the last minute, seemed to never be enough. I had to pretend that his secret escapades didn't exist—finding lipstick stains on the collars of his white shirts, saturated with *Shalimar*.

He always found something wrong with my chores and punished me by suspending my calls to my parents and Geraldine. There were times when he locked me in the basement overnight without food and appropriate toileting. I had to use a bucket to relieve myself and tear off newspaper pieces to wipe.

The best thing about Jimmy Lee being a salesman was he'd need to travel several times a year out of state for a week at a time. I breathed easier and called my friend, Ethel, from across the street during those times. Ethel had befriended me when we first moved into the neighborhood.

I never spoke of my prison life to her, but I think she figured it out after running into me at the grocery store one day. She grabbed me by my arms to hug me. I jumped and turned to face her.

"Why on Earth are you wearing sunglasses on a cloudy day?" she asked, snatching them off my face and laughing. Immediately, my hands flew up to shield my black eye.

"Oh, Val ... is Jimmy Lee hurting you?" she asked, tearing up.

I didn't say anything for a moment. "Clumsy me, I ran into a door a few nights ago," I murmured.

She handed me my glasses back and never questioned me again.

My phone rang Friday night as I was wringing the mop out in the kitchen. I leaned it against the stove and picked up the receiver. "Hello," I said.

"About time you got done," Ethel replied.

I looked over my shoulder and saw her sitting on her patio, smoking. Her patio faced my kitchen and driveway. She waved, and I waved back.

"I thought you quit," I said.

"Me too. Are you busy tomorrow night?" she asked.

"Ethel, you know the answer to that," I said.

"I'm inviting a few of the girls over Saturday night for

dinner and games. Wanna come over?" she asked, tapping her ashes into an ashtray.

"I don't think so. I've got a lot to do around here," I said, squatting down to pick up the mop bucket to empty out.

"Hey, Jimmy Lee is still out of town, right?" she asked.

"Yes," I said. He didn't like me leaving the house even when he was away. Heck, he wasn't due back until late Sunday night. Ethel had invited me other times, and I'd always made up an excuse how I couldn't come over, but not this time. "You know what? Count me in," I said.

"Great, bring my favorite, and I'll have plenty of desserts," she replied, hanging up the phone.

Jimmy Lee was traveling to Maine and Vermont in late September with a return date of October eighth—five days before the annual county fair. I prepared a huge pot roast with all the fixings; I stored half in the fridge for his dinner the next night.

Ethel had invited a few of her friends over. All of their husbands were on a hunting trip that weekend. We ate, drank wine, laughed, and played charades most of the night.

As I was taking the last bite of pie, I saw headlights in my peripheral vision. Ethel looked at me. I froze for a few seconds and flew to her door as the plate landed on her carpet. I knew it was his black Thunderbird. Jimmy Lee had arrived a day early.

Ethel's friends were in the kitchen, cackling, drinking, and probably gossiping about everybody, including us. I reached for the handle of her patio door. She placed her hand on top of mine.

"Val, stay," she pleaded.

"You know I can't do that. He'll find me wherever I am. Your place would be the first place he'd look. It won't stop him," I said with a sigh, looking away from her towards the car. I felt my heart beating fast.

"Don't you think it's time to call the police?" she asked.

"No! That would only make things worse for me, Ethel. Jimmy Lee knows most of the cops on the force." I took my heels off, holding them in my right hand.

"Call me when you can," she requested.

"I'll try when he's not around. It may be a few days," I said. I hugged her tighter than I ever had, as if I knew this would be the last time I would see my friend. I swung the patio glass door open. I wobbled over her freshly cut, damp grass to my backyard as fast as I could, cupping my hand under my round six-month-pregnant belly—the little one kicking me from both sides.

I slid the patio door open to enter our home. A sharp sting landed on my face. He jerked the curtains closed. "Haven't I've told you more than once to stop hanging around with that hussy?" he shouted. His chest puffed out. He rolled up his white dress shirt sleeves and loosened his tie.

"Jimmy Lee, don't call her that. Ethel is the only friend I've made since we moved here," I said, backing up from him and rubbing the side of my face.

"Why are you always talking back to me, woman? You know that pisses me off," he screamed. He charged at me like a bull being released from its caged pen. He pushed me down with his open hands.

I fell backwards, slid on the wood floor in the living room, and slammed up against a standing lamp. I heard the glass shatter and saw his foot rising up to kick me in my abdomen. I tried to block his kicks, cradling my belly to protect my unborn child. I tucked my legs in a fetal position. His foot landed on my back. I started coughing uncontrollably.

"Jimmy Lee, please stop! You're hurting me and our baby. Please ... please!" I begged as tears streamed down my face.

He bent down, grabbed my ponytail, and dragged me across the ground onto the yellow and white kitchen floor. He yanked a cabinet door open and slid some pots towards me. "I've had a tough few days, and I've been driving all morning and most of the night. I'm tired and hungry. I don't ask you for much. You still can't do the easiest job around here— cooking me a good hot meal," he rattled off, clicking his teeth.

"I'm sorry, Jimmy Lee," I yelped.

Breathing heavily and bending over me with his hands on both of his knees, he said, "No, you're not. You love making me upset. I don't want to do these things to you, Val. You just keep pushing me."

I didn't respond to him right away. My head and back were throbbing, and I placed my hand on my back to rub it.

"Didn't you hear me?" he asked, standing over me with his arms crossed.

Glancing up at his lower arm, I noticed his skull tattoo with knives piercing its pulsating red eyes staring down at me.

"Yes, I heard you," I said, taking in deep breaths.

"Good. Now, I'm going go in there to take a bath. When I return, my dinner better be on the table, if you know what's good for you. We have an understanding, right?" He stood up and brushed his hands through his hair.

I tried to pull the loose strands of my hair out of my face with my quivering hands. Attempting to lift myself up off the floor with my elbows and hands, I noticed blood spiraling down my arms.

"I'm waiting," he demanded, tapping his polished loafers against the wood floor.

"Yes, your dinner will be ready before you're done," I stated one word at a time.

"That's more like it. By the way, we're moving soon to a more secluded area where I won't have to worry about nosy Ethel. Earle has some available land out by his place that I've been checking out," he said.

He turned around and ambled down the hallway towards

our bedroom. I pulled myself up using the counter to steady myself. I stumbled over to the kitchen sink and turned on the faucet to run cool water over my hands, hoping to loosen the glass specks and stop the bleeding.

Afterwards, I rinsed my face and patted it dry with the end of an apron hanging on a cabinet knob. I continued crying and glanced down. I slid my hand down to massage my stomach and whispered, "You okay in there? I promise you that one day I'm going to find a way to get us away from him. I just don't have it figured out yet." I didn't know if I was carrying a boy or a girl. I believed it was a girl because of the last thing my grandmom told me. I felt her kick me three times, and I exhaled.

I knew that I didn't have a lot of time before he'd return. I warmed the pot roast that I'd saved earlier in the oven. I washed all the dishes and put them up—one of Jimmy Lee's rules was to not have anything out in the kitchen. As I placed the bottle of Joy dishwashing detergent in the cabinet above the kitchen sink with my trembling hands, it fell and knocked over a container in the back.

Picking the bottle up, I noticed that the container was Folsom Rat Poison. I read the ingredients and cast my eyes on the baking dish inside the oven. I thought to myself, *Just sprinkle a few teaspoons of the powder in his mash potatoes and gravy and mix it up really well*. I placed the box back in its proper space and slammed the door.

Jimmy Lee had never returned home early. After tonight, I knew I could never depend on his schedule. After he ate his dinner and I cleaned up, he fell asleep on the couch in the living room. I drew myself a warm bath and poured the recommended amount of Rexall Epsom Salts in the tub. I unbuttoned the side of my plaid maternity dress, and it dropped to the floor. I peeled off my undergarments one by one.

Staring at my naked body in the mirror, I kneaded my lower back with my hands and turned to the side. I noticed light purple and pink bruises starting to appear in those areas. I stood there for over five minutes and thought how I was lucky this time to have guarded my baby, but what about the next time? I stepped into the warm water and grabbed the rims of the tub with both my hands to lower myself down to soak. Closing my eyes tight, I knew no one could save us from Jimmy Lee, but I made a wish that night anyhow.

The morning of October thirteenth arrived almost overnight, and I couldn't wait for the county fair. This was the one time out of the year other people would admire my talents and praise me for my efforts. I baked cherry and strawberry cobblers that morning. I'd placed third last year at the fair. I was hoping for first place this year. I packed them in the backseat of the car. Jimmy Lee stared at himself in the sideview mirror and stroked his slick hair back with his hand as he lit a cigarette.

I opened up my car door and backed up my rear end on the passenger side. My saddle shoes slipped on some loose gravel. I ended up flopping down in the seat.

"You really need to stop eating so much of the pink pineapple sherbet. I'm going to have to strap you on the hood soon," Jimmy laughed, stroking the arm of his chocolate leather jacket. He placed the car in reverse and headed towards the fairgrounds.

"Jimmy Lee, you missed the street we're supposed to turn on," I said.

He took out another cigarette and lit it up.

"Can you wait until we're not in the car to smoke? I don't want to smell like smoke when the judges are interviewing me," I said, rubbing my belly. The baby started kicking. I reached over to grab his hand and was about to place it on my stomach.

He yanked it back and growled, "What are you doing?"

Smiling and facing him, I said, "She's kicking. Don't you want to feel?"

"No! For all I know, that thing you're carrying may not even be mine," he said, slanting his eyes at me.

"First of all, she's not a thing! Of course she's yours. You're the only guy I've ever been with." My heart started pounding.

Cutting his eyes at me, he said, "Yeah, yeah ... tell me anything. How do I know you're not sneaking around with some fella in the neighborhood that Ethel introduced you to when I'm out of town?"

His eyes seemed to transform to black pearls for a moment.

"You know that's not true," I cried out. My eyes started watering.

"I guess we'll just have to wait until the little brat gets here to see if it looks anything like me," he said with a snicker.

Under my breath, I mumbled, "I hope we're gone by then." I turned away from him and looked out the window.

"What did you just say?" He snatched my face toward him.

"I didn't say anything," I replied, biting the side of my lip.

He slammed on the brakes. I extended my arms to the dashboard to brace myself. He came to a complete stop in the middle of the road as cars honked and passed us by. Jimmy Lee leaned over to me and placed the palm of his hand over my tummy. He started pressing down hard. "Now, we can do this my way or yours. You tell me what you said, and I'll release my hand. You continue to play dumb as you truly are, then the baby may come very early or not at all."

I cringed and screamed out, "Ouch! You're hurting us. I just said if we're gone ... the baby and me."

He started releasing his hand. He raised it up and back-handed me near the corner of my mouth. I collapsed into the window, hitting my head. I felt something salty in my mouth. My hand fumbled around for my purse. I opened it up and pulled out a handkerchief. Holding it close to my mouth, I spit out a pool of blood.

"You're not going anywhere until I say so," he hissed.

"Why do you hate me so much, Jimmy Lee?" I stared at him with tears rolling down my cheeks.

He didn't answer me. He released his foot off the brake and continued to drive. He turned on Emerald Green 377 Country Road. I knew where we were headed now, and it wasn't anywhere near the fairgrounds. Jimmy Lee's friend—Earle Gaines—lived out this way.

Earle was nearly eighty years old and owned a double-deck houseboat and several acres around the lake. No one lived close to him. Five-foot white wooden blood drop crosses and **NO COLOREDS WELCOME** homemade signs decorated the entrance of his property and walkway. Battle worn Confederate flags waved from the roof of his house. I'd never understood what drew Jimmy Lee to Earle until today.

Only, if Earle knew the truth about Jimmy Lee, Earle would grab his rifle from behind his chipped rocking chair and load him up until he'd spent every bullet. Jimmy Lee and I were extremely fair-skinned and easily passed for white in Earle's working-class world ran by the richer Earles. Nobody ever questioned, which provided Jimmy Lee more leeway to do whatever he wanted to others, specifically me.

Jimmy Lee parked the car and stepped out to greet Earle on his porch. Earle pushed himself back and forth on the swing. I didn't move. I could feel my mouth swelling.

They talked for over twenty minutes. Earle left Jimmy Lee and used his staff to climb one step down at a time towards me. Jimmy Lee opened Earle's screen door and entered. Dirt and grease covered the mid-section of Earle's shirt. He approached my side of the car, then partially bent down and tapped the window with his staff, motioning me to roll it down.

"Well, hey there, little lady," he said, his eyes squinting. "You need some ice for that?"

"No, thank you," I replied.

"Listen here, you gotta stop being difficult with my friend. He won't hurt you as much if you stay in line," he said with a crooked grin. "The late Mrs. Gaines, rest her poor soul, used to try to be independent like you, but she knew her place after the first few times. It seems like you haven't learned just yet. Don't worry, you will soon enough, and if not, well ... let me stop yakking," Earle said. He stood up.

The sun was about to set, and the night would follow. Two tall lights on Earle's property lit the deck to a small motorboat. Earle's houseboat sat in the middle of the lake, probably over a thousand feet from his home.

"Jimmy Lee got a surprise for ya out on my boat, there," he mumbled, pointing to the boat. "I think you're gonna really like it. I'll chauffeur you both out there when Jimmy is ready and leave you two lovebirds alone."

Taking in a few deep breaths, I gripped the door handle tight. Earle traveled down to the dock. Jimmy Lee was pacing on the porch with something behind his back. He looked up at me. He descended down the steps without taking his eyes off me. It was the same look he'd had when we first met at the school dance.

We'd slow danced to every song, regardless of the song being a love ballad by Nat King Cole or a fast one by Elvis. Ms. Crenshaw, the lead chaperone, kept a close eye on us that night, tapping her ruler in the palm of her hand and adjusting her eyeglasses, until Jimmy Lee asked me if I wanted to go park on

Cypress Hills. Before we left, I told Geraldine where I was going.

He picked me a handful of wildflowers, my favorite, and placed two on each side of my pigtails. We made out in the back of his car—first time I ever did anything like that with a boy. He tried to go further than second base, but Geraldine tapped on the fogged car window just in time.

Catching my breath, I rolled it down. She told me that my dad was driving around town asking where I was. I kissed Jimmy Lee and hopped out of his car to jump into Geraldine's brother's car. I thought about Jimmy Lee all night. We started courting a few days after the dance. I don't know what it was, but Jimmy Lee always had a way of placing me in a trance early on, to the point where all the bad things that were a part of him temporarily vanished.

I heard Earle whistling from a distance and saw Jimmy Lee approaching the car door with a rainbow of wildflowers. He handed them to me; he knew all of my weaknesses. My hand reached for them. My face found comfort from the flowers' damp coolness. "You remembered," I said as tears pooled in my eyes.

"Of course. You thought I forgot about our anniversary?" he asked with a slight grin and tucked his hands in his pants. He opened the door and extended his hand and said, "I have something really special to show you on the houseboat. Come."

"What about the fair?" I asked.

"We can go some other time," he whispered.

My brain told me to stay exactly where I was. The keys were in the ignition. All I had to do was slide over to the driver's seat, start the car up, and drive as far as I could. I could leave him with Earle and never look back. However, my heart told me to go see what Jimmy Lee had planned for our anniversary. I paused for a minute and chose to take a chance with my heart.

He touched the back of my hand as we headed down to the end of the dock. Initially, my hand retreated from his. He pressed his lips against my fingers, kissing them lightly. "Val, I love you so much."

I couldn't respond.

He looked into my eyes and said, "It's okay. I understand. Just wait until you see what I planned for you." He went down the ladder first and then helped me down into the boat, his hands firmly gripping my waist. Earle started the engine, and we shot off. Cool water sprayed lightly against my face and arms. The sunlight was fading, and I noticed a shooting star fly overhead.

When we arrived at the houseboat, I noticed a picnic basket with yellow rose petals and a bottle of wine sitting in the middle of a checkered red and black blanket with pillows. Earle dropped us off. "I'll see you two kids later," he said and snickered under his breath. He blew smoke out of his wood pipe and rolled his red knit cap down over his ears with his hand.

Earle sped off. Jimmy led me inside the boat and helped me sit down on one of the oversized pillows. He fed me shrimp cocktail and gazed into my eyes as he poured two glasses of white wine. He handed me a chilled glass.

I took a few sips and folded my hands in my lap.

He handed me a tiny white box with a red ribbon tied around it.

Staring down at the gift, I thought about all the other gifts he'd given me.

"Open it already," he commanded.

I knew what that meant, so I placed my wine glass on the ground next to me. Without another delay, I prepared to open it. Tears flowed from my eyes.

"Hey, what's the matter?" he asked, stroking the side of my face and pinning my hair back behind my ear.

Wincing and pulling back, I asked, "Why are you always hurting me, Jimmy Lee?"

He placed his wine glass next to him and replied, "Look, Val, I know I can be difficult to live with sometimes. I'm sorry for what I did to you a few nights ago and earlier today. I don't want to hurt you. You just make me so crazy sometimes that I don't know how to control my temper. I'm really sorry. You believe me, right?"

"Jimmy Lee ...," I said in a trembling tone.

"You don't have to answer that now, just finish opening up your gift." He turned away to refill his glass.

I untied the ribbon with a sigh. A gust of wind captured the ribbon, carrying it out of my sight. I noticed shimmering purple and lime-green lights out on the lake. "Jimmy Lee, do you see the lights?" I asked, pointing in front of me.

He shifted his head around to where I was directing him. "Nope ... I don't see anything out there."

My attention returned to the gift, and I opened the box. I lifted it up. It was a heart-shaped emerald on a white gold necklace.

"Oh, Jimmy Lee, this is really beautiful," I said, placing the box in front of me.

"Let me put it on you," he requested, drinking down his wine.

"It's no hurry," I said, placing the necklace back in its box.

"You don't like it, Val?" he asked, clicking the glass with his finger.

"No, no ... I just thought I would wear it when we go somewhere special," I said.

Taking in some deep breaths, he said, "This is special. Right here. Tonight. Hand me the necklace."

With jittery hands, I lifted the necklace back out of the box and handed it to him.

He pulled my hair up with his free hand and fastened it around my neck. "You love it?" he asked.

"Yes, I do," I said in a low tone.

"How much do you love me?" he asked.

"You know how much," I replied, holding in my tears.

He embraced me tight and kissed the side of my neck and whispered, "I got one more big surprise for you." He scooped me up into his arms and carried me over to the other side of the boat.

My arms draped loosely around his neck. He carried me towards the back of the boat. "What's the surprise?" I asked, looking around—there was only darkness and cool winds blowing through my hair as he set me down.

"This," he said, pointing at something that resembled a square waterhole in the houseboat.

"How is this a surprise?" I questioned. The hairs on the back of my arms started tingling. "Jimmy Lee, I want to go home ... let's go home," I begged.

He paced around me and stopped when he was behind me. Before I could turn around to say something else, he'd grabbed a pair of handcuffs with a rope tied to one of the cuffs; a burlap bag hung from it. He cuffed my right arm. I tried to pull it over my wrist.

"What are you doing?" I squealed. I scanned the ground for something to pry the cuff off my arm with. There was nothing near me. "Jimmy Lee, please unlock this!" I yelled out.

Before I could jump into the lake, he shoved me down into the hole. I grabbed one of his hands. I hung on to his wedding ring finger, digging my nails into his skin. He pried my fingers apart, yet I managed to rake it off. I screamed before I went under. A few drops of his blood floated down past me.

Water immediately entered my nose. I tried to keep myself

afloat in the confined area and pull myself up from the edge, but whatever was in the bag was pulling me down fast. Plus, the pressure from his hand pushing me under and his fist beating on my fingers as I tried to hold on to the edges. I struggled to bop my head up for a few seconds, spitting up water and crying simultaneously.

"Why, Jimmy Lee?" I asked, attempting to tread water. The weight of the bag was dragging me under more.

"I told you not to get pregnant again," he sneered. "I never wanted children. You defied me." He continued to press down.

I screamed as loud as I could, choking on the water going down my windpipe.

"Scream all you want, Val. No one is going to hear you out here," he said with a sinister grin sculpted on his face. "Earle told me to take care of you before now, but I didn't. He was right about you trapping me."

I tried to hold my breath as long as I could, protecting my baby, but I was losing my battle. Before everything went completely black, I felt spiky fish fins brush up against my dangling legs. I looked down, trying to make out what it was. With the dark water and my dwindling vision, I was unable to identify it. I couldn't see Jimmy Lee's face anymore. I knew I was *dying*. Something slimy wrapped around my feet and dragged me deeper to the bottom of the lake.

Waking up face down on the ground, the honey-amber sunrise was nearly complete. I opened my eyes, and blood was everywhere on the deck. I jumped halfway up and noticed blood on my dress and hands. My breathing picked up. I saw Earle's broken pipe and his stocking cap ripped in pieces, floating in the lake. Jimmy Lee's jacket was torn to shreds and scattered around me. I called out to Earle and Jimmy Lee. They didn't answer back. I stood up and immediately fell back down—my legs rubbery. *What did I do?* I started weeping.

You're probably not going to believe what I'm about to tell you, and what I saw rising out of the lake. The deck rippled under me, and my body lifted a few inches off the ground. I scooted backwards as far as I could, my heart racing.

The creature was over nine feet tall, with deep purple crystal-like skin and glowing antlers adorning its head like a crown. Black, iridescent fins layered all over its body. Its turquoise octagonal eyes focused on me.

I blinked a few times and placed my hand on my stomach and felt all around. Nothing ... no kicking. I started crying because I knew that I'd lost another baby. The creature flew from the water towards me. Any ordinary person would've run; not me. I'd already been dealing with a *monster* for a long time. The only thing left was for it to kill me, and I'd been nearly there just a few hours ago. It knelt in front of me. Its blood-stained claws hovered over my stomach. An intense blue glow emerged, and I felt my baby kicking again. I looked into the creature's eyes and mouthed, "Thank you."

Its fins rolled back over its abdomen. The creature was also pregnant. It pointed at the car and levitated back over to the water. It tapped something on its wrist fin, rocketed up in the sky with its arms stretched out, stopped mid-air, and dove down into the lake without a splash, then vanished.

I kept my eyes on the water for a few minutes before I stood up. I jerked the necklace from around my neck and chucked it into the lake—it was only Jimmy Lee bait like all the other times. I marched over to the car and got in. I had a story to make up about what happened to Jimmy Lee and Earle and a baby to deliver in three months.

Adjusting the rearview mirror, I noticed the swelling and bruising around my mouth were untraceable and the aching from my back had stopped. I rolled my window down and bent over to do the same with the passenger window. I felt something partially wet touch my side. It was a pair of overalls, shirt, and cotton satchel on the seat. I untied the bag and peeked inside—it was full of cash. I looked all around me and focused on the lake to see if I could see anything ... no trace of my hero. I recalled what I did that night in the bathroom—this was confirmation and, finally, our *freedom*.

I started the car up and hightailed it away from there. A few miles down the road, I heard a loud explosion and saw smoke coming from Earle's place in the rearview mirror. I smiled and kept driving to the airport to purchase my one-way ticket to Puerto Rico.

The radio turned on by itself—a neon blue light emitted from it. The dial started zipping right and left on its own until it landed on a specific station. "Long Tall Sally" by Little Richard blasted from the speakers.

A Woman's World

By Rebecca Evanesky

Julie Bowery stared up at the ceiling of the seedy hotel room. The musty, warm feel with the scent of afternoon passions and body sweat still hung in the air. Her auburn hair was splayed around the pillow behind her head like a halo. Her eyes tracked the smoke from her cigarette as it rose up in the stale room. She sighed, extinguishing her cigarette in the white ashtray resting on her stomach. It rose and fell with each breath, standing in stark contrast to her black slip and matching bra.

The bathroom door opened, and she shifted her gaze. In silence, she watched as her boss and lover, Frank Holcomb, buttoned up his dress shirt, then crossed the room to his shoes. He was a lean, handsome, and bookish looking man in his mid-forties. Julie admired him, though some might consider him past his prime. Every week for the past seven years, they met at the same hotel right off the highway on a desolate back road. A place used for hideaway lovers and passing travelers.

To see them together, one would never guess they were lovers. Julie was vivacious and attractive. The way she wore her hair and heavy makeup were not indicators of wealth, as some might think. Frank, the prominent business owner, carried himself as shy, quiet, and reserved. He came from old money with a well-to-do name. He lived a country club life, complete with a socialite housewife and two fine children. Emily, his daughter, planned on graduating from high school. She was sure to meet her future husband at one of the country club events later that summer. Frank's son, Kenyon, who was twenty-one, was getting ready to graduate from the university. Afterwards, he wanted to follow in his father's footsteps and work at a law firm. Frank had the perfect life, at least that's how Julie thought of it.

Which made it all the more surprising when he would look at her with hungry eyes as she dropped files off at his desk. The looks graduated to sideways glances in the break room and cute jokes around the office. These then culminated in him inviting her to lunch. She remembered being too nervous to eat her chicken salad that day, but not too nervous to meet him back at the same hotel they were in now.

"Can't stay too late," Frank said, pulling Julie from her thoughts. "I've got a meeting with Jack Bishop and then golf. Don't stay too late, or there will be talk in the office." He didn't wait for her to answer. He was out the door without looking back.

There was no kiss on the cheek ... hell, he didn't even blow her a kiss. It had been this way for the last year and a half. She couldn't shake the lingering, sickening feeling this created in her over the past eighteen months. Julie saw the signs. She knew he was losing interest and there was nothing she could do to stop it.

Her thoughts drifted back to the start of their affair. How she had felt overwhelmed and flattered but also scared. She never wanted to break up Frank's marriage. What she felt had nothing to do with his family. Over time, she understood why he was doing this with her. Julie told herself it was all about playing the social game. Frank wasn't getting what he needed at home. He still loved his wife, so it wasn't about something so gregarious. It was about lack. Julie felt as though she were giving him something special, something he couldn't ask of his dear wife—she was such a lady and would cringe at what the two of them did in the bedroom.

The degrading sex was fun at first. It wasn't until later Julie would feel the brunt of the facts. Frank had no problem asking her for what he wanted, whether she liked it or not. Frank didn't give a shit about Julie being the other woman. She pushed it all out of her mind as she made her way back to the office.

It was around 2:00 p.m. by the time she got back to the office. Somehow, she managed to find time to bring a ham sandwich and a nectarine from the automat on the way. She would eat it at her desk while she finished typing reports.

She cringed, thinking about her workload. *Ugh, so many reports to finish.* The disgust in her thoughts became visible on her face. She flared her nostrils and bit down hard. She wanted to explode in a fit of profanity, but such outbursts were not becoming of a lady. *We slave over these reports. All of us women. For what? Only for the men to get the credit.*

Such things used to not bother her. Today, however, she felt like she teetered on the edge of madness. Life brought with it certain revelations at times. And the reality of the situation between her and Frank screamed at her. She couldn't fool herself any longer, and it infuriated her.

She passed Miss Grimes, the head secretary, on her way to

her desk. She'd heard rumors Miss Grimes was once an incredible beauty, a favorite among the bosses in her day. Now in her mid-60s, they ignored and avoided her. She had never married and was forever working at the office. Julie wasn't stupid. She sensed they were trying to push Miss Grimes out to retirement. The new hire made it obvious—Peggy Steele, the young and beautiful vivacious blonde.

Julie arrived at her desk and sat down. *Dear God,* she thought. *Here we go again. Disgusting pigs. All of them.* She watched as the older men leered down at Peggy, putting their arms around her and calling her an asset. The urge to eat evaporated, and Julie wanted to puke.

Peggy's slight smile, glowing with pride, changed in the blink of an eye as a hand crept down her back to her ass. Miss Grimes saw it too. Her expression was a concoction of anger and sadness. It told Julie she understood what was happening and made Julie wonder if there wasn't a hint of jealousy.

Julie caught her own reflection in the window. It was frightening to see herself between Peggy and Miss Grimes—a young, beautiful girl and an old, motherly woman. The scene made her shudder.

She pulled her attention away from the reflection when Frank came strolling by with the other executives. They all beamed at Peggy. The head boss, an old marshmallow kind of man with undertones of sleaziness waiting to break out, put his arm around Peggy. Something about the gesture revolted Julie. The boss seemed to hold Peggy like she was some sort of possession.

Julie had heard tales about the old sleaze being a womanizing buffoon. It made her glad Frank had picked her up first instead of the boss or one of the other men. Julie knew herself by now. She didn't trust she wouldn't have gone along with anything an older man wanted her to do. She would have made the sacrifice in order to have a family.

"I want to have your attention," Mr. Chambers, the marshmallow boss, said to the entire room. "Come August, we will have a brand-new head receptionist." He held his hand out. "Miss Peggy Steel, who has proven to be an incredible asset, even at the tender age of twenty." He looked over at Miss Grimes with sad eyes. All for show, of course. "We will miss the orderly structure of our dear Miss Grimes, as she is off to enjoy her golden years of retirement."

The room resounded with whispers and murmurs. The news came as a surprise. Miss Steele had only been there a few months. Julie examined the room. The scowls on the other women's

faces gave their anger away. And why wouldn't they be livid? Most of them had been there longer and were more qualified for the head secretary position.

Julie understood the women's contempt. Her wrath wasn't directed at the young girl. Instead, she glared at Mr. Chambers, Frank, and the other male executives.

Disgusting pigs, Julie thought. *Pitting woman against woman. Those bastards! No camaraderie. God forbid any sisterly camaraderie. They always think with their cocks, pushing the prettiest and youngest out front like prized possessions.* This was why after every business trip, the girls came back looking frazzled, downcast, but wearing new jewelry.

It infuriated and grieved her at the same time. Julie's body shook with a sad shudder. Frank hadn't given her anything new in a long time. Not even flowers or a single, solitary rose.

Julie was approaching forty. Frank often used the rhythm method, but twice there had been "accidents." Julie was still amazed that Frank just happened to know a doctor friend whom he knew to call. Given the time, she had to wear a blindfold, so she was never really sure how they got to the office and she had never seen the doctor's face before—he always had a mask on when she saw him. The first time, Frank stayed nearby, gave her flowers, candy, and let her take the next few days off, and even checked in on her.

The second time, Frank seemed annoyed that it happened again. It was about three years after her last one. It was similar to before, only Frank didn't stay; he dropped her off with that masked doctor alone, again, not sure where she was. He came to pick her up two hours later, but he didn't stay. Not even when she had more bleeding than usual. Frank was cold and distant when he picked her up; he even told her to be at the office the following morning, even though she was still cramping and bleeding.

Then there was the day Julie's typist, Marie Hatcher, walked past Frank. She saw Frank's eyes follow Marie just as they had her when she was a temp. Even before Marie, Julie could see the vicious cycle. She chose to ignore it then. Yet the game never stopped. These male dogs acted no better than hounds, looking for the next bitch in heat to sniff.

At the end of the day, after the men had their congratulatory celebration for Peggy, they invited Peggy and the new temps to go to a back room and indulge in alcohol.

The drinking at the office had been going on for a while. Julie didn't say a word when she went in to hand the papers for them to sign. They ignored her, treating her as if she were

invisible. She could have walked in naked, tits flopping everywhere, and they would have been none the wiser.

Their lack of acknowledgement made her feel dirty, used, and thrown aside. Mr. Chambers, the old men, and even Frank—they had no more use for her. She wasn't a youthful twenty-something; she was a worn-out wineskin. Julie did her best to conceal the disgust on her face.

"Boy, I tell you, it's nice to finally get rid of that old hag Grimes. Having some fresh blood up front should prove pretty effective and retain clients," one of the old men said, his bald head glistening under the light.

"Man, if I had to come in and look at Grimes every day compared to Peggy, I would run," another one of the men said. He slapped his hand on the table, and his double chin flopped with laughter.

Julie forced herself to stop listening when they started to make gestures with their hands about Peggy's body. She pitied the girl. She knew what came next for her. These vile creatures saw her as nothing more than an object. The same with Martha. Miss Grimes was more than a clump of aging skin and bones these cretins had reduced her down to. But these buffoons never took note of it.

The men signed the documents, and Julie returned to her desk. While she covered her typewriter, she saw Martha gathering up her things for the weekend.

"Why don't we have a farewell party tonight before you leave next week? Just us ladies?" Julie blurted it out before thinking. It seemed like the right thing to do.

Martha looked out at Julie, every muscle in her face flexed into a joyous expression. "Oh, Julie. That would be lovely! Thank you."

Less than an hour later, all of the "older" women from work were camped out at a bar near the office.

"I can't tell you how many times I went down on that bald fuck in my youth," Martha said, nursing a gin and tonic. "Hell, I even perfected a method where I could take both balls of his in my mouth at the same time." She held out her hand, making a cupping gesture. "In my prime, he wouldn't have been able to keep his hands off me." She grew somber, set down her glass, and seemed to stare at nothing. "And then, little by little, he made it clear how much I didn't matter to him."

Martha had needed the job. She thought Chambers would respect her ... or at least see her as an equal. "The last time we were together was almost ten years ago." Martha finished off her drink. "That was when he told me some line about how men either respect a woman or they accept her, but never both." She gave a mocking laugh. "I knew at that moment what he really thought of me. I've been looking for other jobs ever since. Got this job at the library near my sister and my daughter. Less pay but should be a bit more pleasant."

Julie's eyes widened. She knew the daughter Martha spoke of. It was the one she'd had with Mr. Chambers.

Martha told them the story about when she got pregnant. It was right after she had started working for Chambers thirty years ago. She had kept it from him, explaining how she didn't want to lose the baby. At the ripe age of twenty, she knew he would force abortion on her.

As Martha talked, Julie thought of Frank. The way he made it sound when he coerced her into the abortion. The entire conversation reminded her of what happened with her aunt. She had watched her struggle for years, then die in poverty. An employer had impregnated her aunt, but she was determined to keep her son no matter the cost.

"I gave birth at my sister's," Martha continued. "My child stayed there with her and my cousins. She knows she's my daughter, but we weren't that close." Martha sighed. "She now has her own family. She offered for me to come stay, but I want my own life."

Tears streamed down Julie's face.

Martha looked at Julie, her eyebrows scrunched together and nostrils flared. "Julie, hon.

What is it?"

Julie spoke so only Martha could hear. "I *knew* mine were a boy and a girl. I wanted to keep them so badly, but my parents are gone. I have no one to help or back me. I could have said that I adopted a child ... but I was *so scared* and ..." She wiped a tear. "In so many words, I was told if I wanted to keep things as they were, I had to ..." Julie looked down at her hands, shaking her head. "So I sacrificed my own children to keep a pathetic man who doesn't even want me anymore." She glanced back up at Martha, ashamed.

Martha gave an understanding nod, placing her hand over Julie's. She sensed the understanding in Martha, though she didn't speak a word.

Martha shook her head and wrapped an arm around Julie. She held Julie as she cried soft whimpers into her neck. The women around them chatted away, taking no notice of their intimate moment.

"It's a disgustingly masculine world," Martha whispered in Julie's ear. "They never understand how much we sacrifice for them. They make us into beings we are not. But it's just so simple. We just want to be loved. We want to be accepted, but they can't comprehend that. For some reason, such a thing cannot be accepted."

The door to the bar opened, and the chattering women around them fell silent. Peggy Steele entered, accompanied by some of her friends.

Some of the older women hurled a few taunts their way. "Is this the welcoming party?"

"What's the matter, honey? They run out of booze at your *other* party?"

Julie watched in silence as the young women made their way to the bar. She studied their faces. Red cheeks, downcast eyes, and quivering lips. Whatever went on in the back room at the office must have been unpleasant.

The younger ladies sat down at the bar next to Julie and Martha. Peggy spoke first. She turned to Martha with tears glistening in her eyes.

"This wasn't what I wanted," she said. "I pleaded with him to keep you on. I needed your help. I know only so much of what I'm doing and ..." She swallowed hard. "I know the price I'll have to pay. They made it abundantly clear tonight." Peggy turned forward, away from Martha and Julie. "My roommate is my best friend from high school," she continued. "Her name is Allison, and she's been like family to me." Peggy grabbed the waitress's attention and ordered a whiskey.

Julie and Martha exchanged sideways glances, their faces wrinkled in confusion, wondering where this conversation was headed.

"I wear professional clothing as a way to fit in," Peggy said, still facing forward. "I went to school for typing and short-hand so that maybe one day, I could be more. Do you know that every night when I go home to Allison, I wish I was a man so I could really be free? Then I could be who I want to be and I wouldn't have to hide Allison as just my roommate."

Julie and Martha eyed each other, smirking. It made sense. Peggy was the only lady in the office to never talk about men. In fact, Julie couldn't recall a time she ever saw a male visit her at

work, only Allison. Then there was the uptight, uncomfortable body language she displayed around men.

Peggy took a sip of the whiskey she'd ordered. "I made the mistake of confiding in a man about who I am only once. He was almost excited and ecstatic at the prospect of having two women in bed." She chuckled. "Can you believe that? It's *my* sexuality. It's what I want. I'm not here to be a man's fucking ornament; I just want to earn my money and provide for me and my family. I left a good internship once because I was sexually propositioned. I refuse to run again." She raised her glass and finished off the whiskey.

Martha rubbed Peggy's back the way a mother would comfort a child. Peggy turned toward Martha. She pulled Peggy close, holding her as the tears started to flow.

The deep confessions ceased as night wore on, morphing into jokes and laughter. Blowing off steam felt good, yet in between the humor, the anger and sadness over how Chambers and the other men treated them scratched underneath the surface.

Around 11:00 p.m., Peggy, Julie, and Martha finished up their conversation. Julie and Peggy paid the tab, and the three women left together. The dark streets were quiet, the only sound being the chatter of the three women and their heels clicking the pavement. They were chatting about their summer plans when Peggy came to a jarring stop.

"Look, ladies," she gasped. "The shop is open." Peggy pointed off to her right.

"Oh, I don't think we can go in there," Julie said, shaking her head. "I was raised a strict Catholic and warned about these occult shops."

Martha agreed. "Yes, I was raised Catholic too."

They eased towards the door anyway in curiosity. Martha turned to the other two, and with a mischievous smile, said, "Well, ladies, let's go in. It says they're open till one in the morning."

Before Julie could mount a protest, they were standing inside the shop. The place was filled with curiosities from other worlds—objects of peculiar shapes, skeletons, and candles. The smell of incense filled the room. The place stood in stark contrast from the stores they were used to. No one else roamed inside the shop except them, and coming down from the alcohol, they weren't sure what they were looking for.

A vibrant voice resounded from behind them. "May I help you ladies find something?" They turned to see a beautiful dark-skinned woman standing with her arms by her sides and smiling. Her black, curly hair hung over her shoulders. An air of freedom radiated from her presence. It

was a wild beauty each of the women admired. Something like a men's white dress shirt covered her upper body, with a long red skirt reaching to her ankles.

"Hi," Julie said. She wrung her hands, took a deep breath,

and exhaled. "We uh ... just got done celebrating." She glanced at her friends, seeing their downcast faces. "And came to a sad realization about how the world works. Especially with men. On our way home and just decided to step in."

The shopkeeper looked them up and down. "Been a rough night for you ladies?"

This got Martha to open up. "Oh, honey. You have no idea. When you reach my age, you live long enough to watch the men want you, have you, and then toss you. Whether it be in their bed or professionally."

The shopkeeper laughed. "Ah yes, the wonderful, hypocritical, and fragile patriarchy. Even the ones who claim to be the best allies can still turn at the drop of a hat. They always end up focusing on their own needs. It's almost as though men forget that what it takes to be a real woman is that beautiful togetherness. That magical dichotomy of the male and the female blended together."

Peggy furrowed her brow. "What do you mean? I'm confused. We're women, not men."

The shopkeeper nodded. "Yes, but are we not both mothers and fathers? Are we not teachers and laborers? If I may ask, are any of you married?"

The ladies shook their heads.

"So then," the shopkeeper continued, "on your own, how many times have you all had to play plumber? Play the man and be your own protector? Men are threatened by that." She raised an eyebrow. "Men are still boys at heart, and they fear women. Look at history. The women have been the pillars of strength. They have banded together, brought down armies, been the most lethal warriors. Western culture did away with it all."

"Lot of good it does when you're my age," Martha huffed. "Over the hill. No longer considered attractive, this will be it for me until my time is up. I should have left when I was younger and just seen what else could have been for me. It feels like this is it for me."

"I should have moved away, had my babies, then said I was a widow and gone on my own," Julie said, tears welling in her eyes.

Peggy traced her finger over a figure of two females holding hands. "I don't know what I could do to make it easier, other than to hide."

The shopkeeper's eyes widened with empathy. "Ladies, since it has been a difficult night for all of you, may I suggest a gift for you three? It's something I think you should take into your office." She held out her finger. "But only open it when all else fails. When you're ready." Her lips curved into a half smile. "But I think you're there. Just be prepared because after you start this journey, you must finish it." She faced the shelf next to her and removed a book.

Martha reached out a trembling hand and took it.

A cold chill rippled up Peggy's spine, and a strong emotion of caution rushed over Julie.

Martha saw the fear on her friends' faces. "I'll keep it," she said. "I'll know when the time is right."

———

Business went along as usual on Monday. Martha finished up and vanished as fast as possible. Peggy tried to hide her lack of confidence, knowing at any moment, someone would see how unqualified she was to take over Martha's position.

Everything rolled along status quo for the remainder of the week. Until Frank called Julie into his office Friday morning. She slipped in, wondering what in the hell this was all about. Chambers was there, as was Sterling. Some called Sterling a white-haired silver. Julie saw him as an oversized leprechaun with pointed ears.

"Julie, my girl," Frank said. "You're being promoted. You've been here a while, and you know the company. We consider you too much of an asset to be buried behind a desk with all of us old men. We feel it's best for you to be working with the temps. They need you, and we need you to train them so that we can all work together as a team."

A feeling of disgust washed over Julie. She tried to not let it show on her face. *You all seem to have forgotten all the times I've come in here to have papers signed while you openly talked about the attractive females*, Julie thought. *How you lure in clients. How you even used some of the temps as a way to sign deals.*

"Besides, you're still young enough. You could go find a man to finally settle down with. A girl like you would make a great wife and a great mother," Frank said.

Julie furrowed her brow in anger and flared her nostrils. Frank stared into her eyes, unaware of the fire raging inside.

The prick is clueless, Julie thought. *All he sees is* a body of flesh *he could have his way with.*

The rage. The mistreatment. The way they used her and the rest of the women. It all built up inside Julie like torrent rivers. The dam was about to burst.

Julie placed a hand over her mouth and laughed. It was a menacing laugh, graduating into hysterics.

The men eyed each other, confused. Sterling twirled his finger around his temple and whistled a cuckoo sound.

Chambers grunted and said, "Typical woman response. Get outta here and be ready to go on Monday."

The men rolled their eyes, chuckling as Julie left. She stepped out, her anger beginning to wane, and ran into Martha. She had been standing on the other side of the door. Julie glanced down at her hands to see her holding the book the shopkeeper gave them. Peggy stood beside Martha, and the two were engaged in conversation.

Martha faced Julie.

"What are you doing with that?" Julie asked.

"Chambers is already planning a business trip for he, Peggy, and Allison," Martha said. "It seems he found out about Allison and is encouraging her to come along. Or else he will out them, and you know what that could mean."

"Dear God," Julie said, placing a hand over her mouth.

Martha held up the book. "Ladies, it's time to act. Now. Call me crazy, but the shopkeeper gave us this for a reason. It has to have an answer."

Julie didn't know what the book had to do with any of what happened. She was taken off guard, as if she had just woken from sleep. Whatever was in the book would be like pulling up the shade and letting in light. "Just open the book, Martha. I don't think we have anything to lose."

Martha opened the book.

At first, nothing happened. It was pages of words and symbols. Martha spoke, reciting a line from the book as her hands trembled. Julie didn't sense anything, neither were there any odd feelings. She stared down at the page.

"I think we should—" Julie's words were cut short. She glanced up at Martha and gasped.

Martha's eyes had gone black as night. The hair on her head grew long and turned white. Her beauty remained, and added to it was an exaggerated look of age and wisdom.

Julie's eyes darted to Peggy. The same type of black eyes lay in her sockets. Long brown hair cascaded down her shoulders. There was a youthfulness to her, like a nymph or some other mythical creature.

A sharp pain radiated through Julie's stomach. She glanced down at the round bulge in her belly. She looked pregnant. But how could that be? Her pulse raced, and her hands grew clammy. She caught her reflection in the office window.

"Oh my God," she whispered. Her eyes were as black as

the others. She tried to speak again, but the words flowing out were in a language she'd never heard before. She felt as if her soul were being pressed down into the dark channels of her being. Places she never knew existed inside of her. A total loss of control came over her, as whatever possessed her was now in charge.

A wave of madness flowed over the office. The other women stood up from their desks and gathered around them in a circle, chanting in the same ancient language. Whatever had possessed

Julie, Peggy, and Martha now had control over them.

Martha pointed a bony finger at the executive room. The women sauntered over, their black eyes filled with hatred. Still chanting, one of them flung open the door. They descended on Frank, Sterling, Chambers, and two other executives.

"What the hell is this shit?" Chambers yelled.

The laughter died down when the men saw their eyes. They tried to scatter from their seats, spilling their cocktails all over the table. Several of the women grabbed them and threw them back down in their chairs.

Martha pointed at the men, her eyes wild and full of wrath. Julie rubbed her pregnant belly while the remaining women surrounded them. They began to remove the men's clothing.

Chambers relaxed a little. "Well hell, if this is what you wanted, all you had to do was ask."

Sterling's hard pecker was already visible through his underwear. "Group orgy. This is a first."

"If I would have known this was going to happen today, I would have brought my camera," one of the executives said.

The other executive joined in. "Easy now, ladies. Gotta make this last."

The laughter died down when the women got rough, using the discarded clothing to restrain and gag them.

"Hey! What the fuck!" Frank yelled as one of the women wrapped his underwear around his mouth.

Martha lowered the book. Julie saw an image similar to what they were creating in the office. Julie studied the page ... and it all made sense. Her, Peggy, and Martha were now the Mother, the Maiden, and the Crone. They represented the mother goddess. The ceremony was punishment. Punishment for those who committed offenses to women. The more Martha spoke, the more Julie understood what was said.

Martha told the men they were to be given a heinous chastisement. As they viewed women, so they themselves would become.

Martha handed Peggy a ceremonial blade that had been strapped to the inside back cover of the book, then moved to the center of the room to instruct the others. The women held the men down tighter. Peggy stepped over to Chambers and raised the blade. She brought it down with violent force, cutting Chambers's penis in half as though slicing a hot dog.

Chambers gave a muffled scream through his gag. Sweat poured down his face, and his eyes rolled to the back of his head. His penis pumped out blood as the crimson liquid flowed down the front of his chair.

Peggy worked the knife more, slicing and prying, until Chambers was cut open from his privates to his chest. His entire lower body was painted red in blood. His filleted stomach moved up and down with his breaths. Whatever force possessed the women seemed to be keeping the men alive. Chambers was wide awake, screaming his ass off in pain.

Peggy's hands were covered with Chambers's blood. She crept across the room, a deviant smile on her face. One by one, she performed the same service on each man. When she finished, she passed the knife to Julie.

Julie placed the blade between her teeth, the copper taste of Chambers's blood exploding in her mouth. She went to each man, pulling apart their broken flesh. Julie started with their mangled manhood. Digging her fingers into the opening, she made a ripping motion. She yanked on their genitals, and the testicles fell at her feet.

Julie walked her hands upward to their chest cavity and pried it open. She made sure the opening in the middle was wider than the top and bottom. Gathering up the severed testicles and penises, she peeled the skin off with the knife as if she were peeling fruit. She then pressed the skin in her hands like dough. She worked and worked. molding and crafting the flesh into

multiple clitorises. She took the knife and sliced more flesh from each man. She fashioned labia, along with the opening to a vagina, which expanded from their previous genitals to their stomachs. When Julie was done, the bloodied, mangled flesh was fresh, sore, and ready to be fucked.

The men stared down in horror at their distorted bodies with the gaping vaginas.

Julie didn't know where it came from, but Martha had grabbed a black candle. She lit it and dropped the wax onto their new private parts. She prayed a blessing, asking that the nerve endings come together and heal.

The men's wounds healed in an instant. The blood flow ceased, and taking up each of their bodies from stomach to genital area was a beautifully crafted vagina. Their screams of insane horror died down, changing into exacerbated pants. The panic painted on their faces was glorious to behold. Bulging eyes, burning cheeks, and sweat dripping down their skin.

Julie looked on, smiling. The vaginas began to seep and secrete mucus. The men's breaths began to hitch. The pain in their chests began again. The men writhed, acting as if they needed some kind of release.

In the unknown tongue, Martha told the women,

"Because these men see us as sacks of meat needing to be fucked, this is what they have become."

Peggy walked around the room, picking up the skinned penises and testicles. She arranged them in a circle on the table. Martha handed Julie and Peggy more black candles and lit them. Julie and Peggy poured the wax over the body parts, repeating Martha's words.

While the women chanted, a beast grew from the severed male parts. Black fur horns adorned the demon's head. The face resembled the mixture of a bull and a moose. Gorilla-like arms and hands swayed by the side of its bulky body. Its hooves clicked on the table as it walked, and a massive penis dangled between its horse-like legs. The demon leaped off the table and made its way towards Chambers, snorting and grunting with each step. Chambers and the other men bucked their hips and chests upward, searching for some kind of release.

The demon gripped Chambers's face and spoke in a guttural voice. "At the will of the Mother, the Maiden, and Crone, I will give you release. Over and over again, and you will never be satisfied!"

Tears formed in Chambers's eyes as he watched the demon drop down to its knees. It opened its mouth, and a tentacle-like tongue wiggled out. The demon ran its tongue over the lips of the
vagina, then flickered it over the clitoris. It did this until the internal organs shuddered with orgasms.

The demon arose to its feet, its cock erect. It traced the tip on the new vagina in Chambers's chest. With a savage thrust, the demon plunged inside Chambers. Chambers's eyes bulged for a moment, then his face grimaced in pleasure.

Martha leaned down, speaking in English into Chambers's ear. "As you saw women. Flesh needing to be fucked. That's how you'll be, you gigantic cunt. Never satisfied. Never satiated. As soon as this demon has given you all, you'll want more."

Chambers felt instant relief as the demon pumped and then emptied its seed inside him. The aching, dull throb dissipated, and reality came crashing down on him. The sheer abomination he had become hit him, and panic engulfed his soul. Chambers began to cry.

The demon withdrew its cock. Chambers bucked his hips and lifted his chest, pleading to be fucked. The pain and need for release was back.

One by one, the demon went through all of the men. He mounted them, giving aggressive thrusts, hitting their hearts and lungs. Yet the men begged for more. They were pathetic beings totally given over to the hunger of their bodies. They wanted nothing more than the demon to enter them, extinguishing the dull ache radiating through their midsections.

Martha climbed on top of the table and addressed the women. "My sisters, it's time to leave.

Our work is done. We have a business to run, and we shall run it together."

Julie expected everything to return to normal. But they had made a cruel bargain. This was reality now. They would work as they were, overseeing the women, training them to be dependent only on themselves. Peggy, the lovely Maiden; Julie, the pregnant Mother; and Martha, the wise Crone. They would lead their female workers, the eternal priestesses, while the males existed as flesh for a sex-hungry demon.

A heartfelt "thank you" to the authors who contributed to this debut Vixens ofHorror anthology! Stay tuned for next year's edition by visiting www.unsaintly.com and clicking "Vixens of Horror."

You can also join my mailing list and stay up to date on future releases